Reflections
from a Mud Puddle

Helping Children Cope and Grow

Compiled by Marcella Fisher Anderson
Illustrated by Christopher Wray

Boyds Mills Press

For my grandchildren: Jonathan, Henry, Edith, Christopher, and Benson

—M. F. A.

TO: Beth, Arlynn, & John

—C. W.

My special thanks to the following people who participated in the making of this anthology:

- All of the authors and poets whose contributions made this book possible.
- My advisory committee, gathered informally out of a knowledge, love, and understanding of children's literature: Gretchen Larson, M.L.S.; Franziska van der Schalie, M.L.S.; Janine Obee, M.A.; Joan Fitchet, B.A.; and my daughter, Marcella Distad, M.L.S.
- Sally Niklas, M.A., manager, child life and education at MetroHealth Medical Center, and her child life staff who helped to clarify the foreword to the book.
- Doris Robinson, M.L.S., whose long experience in using stories and poems with children in need of support illuminated and upheld the concepts of this book.
- My grandson, Jonathan Distad, sixth grader, who served as poetry consultant.
- Mary Kobosky, pediatric R.N., for her generous assistance.
- The Monday Night Writers group for constant support.
- Christopher Wray, whose illustrations enliven the text.
- My editor, Beth Troop, who kept me on track and lightened our decision-making with her infectious good humor.
- And finally, loving appreciation to my husband, Glenn, for his insights and encouragement.

—M. Anderson

Text copyright © 1998 by Marcella Fisher Anderson
Illustrations copyright © 1998 by Boyds Mills Press
All rights reserved

Published by Caroline House
Boyds Mills Press, Inc.
A Highlights Company
815 Church Street
Honesdale, Pennsylvania 18431
Printed in China

Publisher Cataloging-in-Publication Data
Reflections from a mud puddle / compiled by Marcella Fisher Anderson ;
illustrated by Christopher Wray.—1st ed.
[96]p. : col. ill. : cm.
Summary: A collection of stories and poems to help children with special needs.
ISBN 1-56397-606-4
1. Children's poetry. 2. Children's stories. [1. American poetry. 2. Stories]
I. Anderson, Marcella Fisher. II. Wray, Christopher. ill. III. Title.
808.8—dc21 1998 AC CIP
Library of Congress Catalog Card Number 97-77905

First edition, 1998
Book designed by Tim Gillner
The text of this book is set in 12-point Garamond.
The illustrations are done with pencil.

10 9 8 7 6 5 4 3 2 1

CONTENTS

AUTHOR'S NOTE

Reflections from a Mud Puddle is a source book to be used by adults. Parents, teachers, caregivers, children's librarians, and all others who work with children will find helpful materials in the form of stories, poems, ideas, and information. In selecting the appropriate materials, trust your own life experiences and intuition, as well as your knowledge of the child or children.

Each of the ten topics used to organize the materials is based on concerns common to many children. A number of contributors and I have experienced the anecdotes describing how particular books have been used in addressing these concerns.

Sometimes the stories will lead to an informal discussion. A relationship—a sense of togetherness between the adult and child—can help to open up a sharing of feelings. The optional questions following the stories are largely open-ended, so that the children will not be anxious about giving acceptable answers. Ideally, the adult should support the children's thoughts and questions as important and natural.

An annotated table of contents is provided for the stories, making it sometimes unnecessary to pre-read them. The detailed and extensive subject index offers further access to the book's contents.

—M. Anderson

FOREWORD

"Stories do more than educate the mind; they also inform the heart."

Bernice E. Cullinan, PhD
Co-author of *Literature and the Child*, Fourth Edition

When children are going through difficult times in their lives—as many are in today's world—often they share similar emotions: anxiety, loneliness, rejection, powerlessness, fear, sadness, and even despair. We know that children believe they are the only ones in their particular situations; the only ones to have certain thoughts and feelings. These feelings can be overwhelming and cause roadblocks in normal growth and development.

In the midst of difficult experiences, children often are more vulnerable than adults, yet they can be highly resilient. Children's natural resiliency can be enhanced by adults who have a relationship with them, who feel with them, and who are attentive to their concerns. One way to help children is to address their concerns through literature—through stories and poems such as those found in this anthology.

If a parent, teacher, or caregiver reads one story or poem that resonates in a child's experience, the child can feel less alone and more affirmed as a person of worth. "When I write for children, I'm trying to tell a child, 'You're valuable,'" says noted children's author Walter Dean Myers.

On the other hand, the stories and poems can be used to help family members, classmates, and friends to understand and relate to a child's situation. As a result, through heightened sensitivities, others may start to offer ways to support the child, to understand, and to extend friendship.

Well-loved author Katherine Paterson has said that good writing helps children "make sense of their own lives." The materials in this book are, first of all, good writing, where the characters grow in maturity. They invite the reader, through imagination, to identify with them, in a sense to become them. The reader or listener believes, "Here is someone much like me, someone who has been where I am."

Recognizing oneself in a character can lower stress levels and diminish isolation. Such recognition can lead to self-discovery and a search for resolutions in a challenging world.

Distinguished author Jane Yolen observes further that some fiction for children "tells us of the world as it should be."

"At the same time," says Sandra Paull, a Winnetka, Illinois, teacher, "a reader or listener can back away from a sensitive issue in a story or poem and take the subject matter merely as part of the story, rather than as personal identification. This possibility is important, too."

The stories and poems in this book honor and respect the child and trust what the child can and wants to take from their content.

The eternal triangle is the reader, the child, the book. Through stories and poems, the lives of children can be enriched, expanded, and empowered. "Tell them stories," says Thomas Thangarad of Emory University. "They stay in their minds as a resource."

Reflections from a Mud Puddle has been compiled with several goals in mind: to support the child; to help share the pain; to affirm the child's worth; to suggest a way toward possible resolutions; to help the child know he or she is not alone; and always to point toward hope—to open the window, and look toward the sun.

CONTENTS (Annotated)

"Coming Around Home": After his mother dies, Jake goes to live with his father whom he barely knows. It is hard for him to leave behind his grandmother with whom he has lived since his mother became ill. When Jake runs away to return to his grandmother, a storm forces him back to his father's house. A turtle and a rock carved with family names help Jake to affirm himself as his father's son.

"The Foster Child" portrays the beginning of a relationship between a pre-teen girl and a newly-arrived foster child of the same age. The situation, concerns, and emotions are realistically portrayed.

"Tire Swing Moments" shows a warm sibling relationship. Especially for the young child, the story points out that tangible reminders of shared past pleasures with a brother or sister can help soothe sad feelings that follow separation.

"The Old Blue Rug": Many times the demise of a pet is a child's first exposure to death. Some of the stages of grief are experienced when a boy's beloved dog dies. A loving family supports the child in working through his sorrow.

"Gabe the Great": An overweight boy who lacks self-esteem has become the butt of teasing and name-calling. At a critical point in a soccer game, Gabe, the third-string goalie, finds himself as the lone defender in a tie-breaking shoot out. Following the game, Gabe shares a moment of triumph with his opponent.

"The Day of the Bamboo Horse": Japanese boys play a game that goes beyond the usual parameters of sport. Players on both sides involve themselves in danger and are aware that their elders would disapprove. Preserving his self-respect through imagining future repercussions, Shigeo respects his oppo-

nent enough to call an end to the game.

"Everybody's Hero" is a vividly written basketball story. Little Man struggles with jealousy as he begrudges his stepbrother's basketball talents. At game's end he is surprised to receive praise from his stepbrother. Talking about the game and the questionable plays leads to a mutual respect and renewed self-respect.

"Joey and the Fourth-of-July Duck" enters the mind of a young child who is developmentally delayed. This story can help raise children's sensitivities to the lonesomeness of a "special child," his efforts to make a friend, and the limited patience of even those who love him.

"Camp Songs": Ellie has a hard time making friends, and they never seem to find Ellie. Why would it be any different at camp? This story relates to children who have feelings of loneliness and believe they lack the skills to make friends, especially when they're away from home.

"Just Like Being There": Due to her chronic illness, Amanda is unexpectedly hospitalized just before her school's championship basketball game. The story illustrates how a close sibling relationship and good friends can help a child in the day-to-day coping with chronic illness.

"Eye Trouble or A Close Encounter of the Nutty Kind" portrays with humor a situation experienced by many children. Becky is already the butt of Jake's constant teasing and is certain that matters will get worse when he learns that she has to wear glasses.

"Playing by the Rules": Sarah has all the attributes of a resilient child—an appealing personality, a loving family, and a supportive community. Her successful effort to participate in her classmates' game of hopscotch points out only one of the many challenges faced by a child with a physical disability.

You Can Do It

"Riding the Wind": Meg has always loved sailing, but a recent serious accident has severely limited her mobility. Her friend Jeff and his father encourage Meg to sail with them. To her surprise, Meg learns that she can still handle a boat and that life may still hold happiness for her.

"Thorgersturm: Voice in the Storm" portrays Marie, a hearing-impaired child. Marie uses her skills in lip reading to save the lives of her schoolmates during a gale off the coast of Scandinavia.

I Did It!

"Two Hundred and Fifty Steps": A young Chinese girl masters her shyness when her mother sends her alone on an important errand. The story rings with the authenticity of daily life in China and focuses on a fear common to many children.

"Fergus Has Spoken!": Fergus Mackey has talked too softly for so long that he thinks he will never be able to speak up. His zany invention leads to a resolution.

That's What Friends Are For

"Nice Guys Win, Too": Ben and his best friend, Wes, compete for the school wrestling championship. In the larger scheme of things, a win for Wes means more than does a win for Ben. Ben's real concern for his friend's welfare dictates the outcome.

"The Homecoming" portrays a reunion between friends. Mary-Margaret's face was burned in an accident, and her best friend worries about seeing her for the first time when she returns home. Will they still be best friends?

Finding Peace—or Making It

"No Man's Land": In the Civil War, Micah, a young Confederate soldier, stands guard so close to the enemy lines that he and Union soldiers can talk together. During a break in the fighting, soldiers from both sides play a game of baseball.

"Neighbors from Cucumbers": A boy named Juan moves in next door to Will. Juan and his parents are migrant workers hoping to settle down for good, but Will notes the lack of welcome toward the new neighbors. It takes an act of overt intolerance to awaken Will and the townspeople to a situation that they have helped to create. In a united effort, they try to make amends.

Tomorrow Will Be Better

"What Will Happen to Dobbie?" is a story about a farm family forced to sell everything at auction. Catherine fears that her pony, Dobbie, will be sold, too, and takes action to prevent it. In so doing, she helps to make the future seem brighter, especially for herself and her grandpa.

"Keeping Snugly Warm": Niki's family is facing hardships. Her father is in the hospital, her mother works the second shift at the diner, and Niki spends long hours alone. The family's problems are not resolved at the story's end, but love and bright stars in the night keep hope alive.

"Angelica's Own Book": The daughter of migrant workers, Angelica has moved from crop to crop and experienced a lifetime of interrupted schooling. Her teacher's special interest in her helps to keep alive Angelica's dream of becoming a teacher herself someday.

Changes in the Family

A six-year-old girl had spent most of her life in hospitals. The longer she was away from her family, the more family bonds weakened. Her parents and older brother visited only twice a year.

In time, her medical condition improved enough for her to leave the hospital. The hospital's children's librarian helped prepare her to return to her family by reading to her. One well-loved book was *Corduroy* (Freeman), the story about a lonely stuffed bear for sale on a department store shelf. When the bear is finally bought by a little girl and carried up her apartment stairs, Corduroy says: "This must be a home . . . I know I've always wanted a home." *Strong character identification* motivated the child's frequent requests to hear this story.

Coming Around Home

By Marcella Fisher Anderson

Jake saw the shadow coming up the walk before he heard the knock. He shivered inside; people knocking at the front door always meant bad news. Not long ago, Reverend Gomes had knocked to tell him that his mother had died.

He watched now as his grandmother opened the screen door. Jake would always remember the flat sound of her voice.

"Jake," she said, opening the door for a tall, weather-beaten stranger, "this here's your father."

Jake stood motionless—like an egret watching fish. His father! After all these years?

Slowly, his father walked into the living room. "Sweet prophecies," he said, looking at Jake. "How you've grown!"

Jake couldn't think of much to say to his father, nor could his father think of much to say to him. They talked very little, even on the long drive inland in his father's pickup truck. Jake just stared at the road as they journeyed away from Tampa and his grandmother's house to Lake Okeechobee and his father's wooden house.

One evening a few weeks later, after a supper of perch and corn cakes, Jake sat on the steps with his father. Not that he especially wanted to—there just wasn't much else to do. They didn't talk; the only sound was the lazy buzz of summer insects. Just then a turtle crawled out of the long shadow of the house.

Jake's father picked it up. "This here turtle has been around for some seventy-five years. He used to sit on a big rock in the stream out yonder. Your great-grandpappy carved his name and his birth date on that rock. Then your granddaddy carved his, too. Later, I carved my own. We were all boys about as old as you."

"Where's the rock now?" Jake asked.

"Covered with water," his father replied. "A few years ago, a flash flood made a new stream bed." Jake's father squinted his eyes at the turtle, then set it down on the sand.

"Will the turtle be back?" Jake asked.

"He'll be back. Just give him time."

Alone all day while his father worked, Jake ached for his mother. He missed his grandmother, too; she always knew when he was hurting and never thought he was too big to hold on her lap.

Finally, Jake decided he couldn't stand it any longer. One hot morning he packed some food in a paper bag and set out for Tampa. His grandmother would sure be happy to see him.

He followed a dry stream bed because he

thought it might lead to Tampa Bay. He stopped at noon under a cottonwood tree and ate some biscuits. The dry, rustling leaves made him sleepy.

When he awoke, the sky was dark and Jake thought he'd better hurry on. Suddenly, rain came. When it pelted down harder, he walked with his head lowered. He didn't see the wall of water rushing down the dry stream bed, hurtling toward him. When he finally realized the danger, it was too late to climb up the bank.

Jake was caught in the churning torrent. He spun around, came up for air, and was dragged down again. Then he let himself be carried along, keeping his head above the water's surface.

Soon, up loomed the cottonwood where he had eaten lunch. He grabbed the lowest branch and swung himself along it, upside down, until he reached dry land. He stood up and looked around. Water squeezed between his toes on the wet sand as the cold rain continued to fall. In the distance, he saw the dull tin roof of his father's house.

Jake blinked. He had come back to where he had started; he hadn't gone anywhere after all.

It was getting on toward evening. The rain finally slowed to a shower. His wet clothes felt chilly and clammy. With a sigh, he turned and started walking in the direction of the house, wading through new stream beds.

The wet, slippery porch rail was still warm from morning. He climbed the steps and turned around to watch the now-gentle rain. The rock was sticking up in a shallow stream, and Jake could see the carved names and dates. He stared at the muddy water swirling around the rock.

He hurried into the kitchen. He didn't know whether his father was home or not, and he wasn't certain he cared. He took a small knife from a drawer and waded to the rock. Silently, he worked on the stone surface.

When he was finished, he returned to the steps and sat down. From the corner of his eye, he noticed his father watching him from the doorway of the house. The man came out and sat down next to Jake.

"I won't ask you where you went or why you came back. It's enough to know you're here," he said. Jake said nothing.

"I was thinking," his father went on. "I could fix up your room and you could camp on the porch. Then your grandmother could come for a visit. Would you like that?"

The steps and rock swam before Jake's eyes. He barely heard what his father said next.

"I haven't been much of a father to you, Jake," he began. "I know that. I was always searching for the big money. When I couldn't make it, I was ashamed to come home to face you and your mother. She was a good woman, and I disappointed her."

Jake turned his head and really saw his father for the first time: the gray-blue eyes—so like his own—looking down at him. Jake spoke slowly, surprised at what he heard himself saying. "We look a little bit alike, don't you think? Maybe a little?"

His father's strong arm pulled him close, then he said, "Sweet prophecies! There's the rock. And you've put your own name and birth date on it! You're some carver there, Jake. The only thing missing now is the turtle."

Jake felt a smile starting. A flow of warmth and happiness spread over his body. "Don't worry," he said. "He'll come around home again. Just give him time."

---

1. Where is Tampa? Lake Okeechobee?

2. Do you follow any traditions in your family that help you to feel closer to one another?

3. How do you think Jake felt when he discovered that he was back at his father's house after the storm?

The Foster Child

By Heather Klassen

I am standing on the front porch, not wanting to go inside. I know the foster child is in there. I guess I should call her by her name.

Lisa. She's twelve, same as me, and her family is going through some hard times. Mom and Dad told me all about her two weeks ago, when they told me they had decided to take in a foster child.

"Sarah, is that you?" My mom's voice floats through the screen door. She's heading my way. But I'm not ready to go in. I dart behind the hedge bordering the porch. My mom pokes her head out the door, doesn't see me, and calls to someone inside. "I guess that wasn't Sarah after all. She should be here any minute."

I plop down beside the bush. I'll have to go inside eventually, but I can't help putting it off. The whole thing doesn't seem fair. When they told me about their foster child idea, Mom and Dad wanted to know how I felt about it. What could I say? Even though I knew it was a nice thing to do, I didn't like the idea of sharing my home—not to mention my parents—with a

stranger. But I don't like to disappoint my parents. So I said it sounded fine, even though it didn't.

Might as well get it over with. I stand up, fling my backpack over my shoulder, and tramp up the steps. Mom meets me at the door.

"There you are, Sarah." Mom holds the screen door open. I step in and glance around the living room. It's empty.

"Lisa's in the kitchen. She'll be out in a minute." Mom puts her hand on my shoulder and leans toward me. "I think she's feeling a little nervous. I'm counting on you to help her feel comfortable, Sarah," she says quietly.

I hear ice cubes clinking into a glass while I wait for Lisa. The questions I've been asking myself for the past two weeks keep circling around in my head. What if she tries to pick fights with me? Or steals my stuff? She's from another part of the city, where no one I know lives. The problems in her family are so bad that she has to live here for a while. Her life sounds so different from mine. What could we possibly have to talk about?

Just as I'm about to ask my mom something, Lisa walks through the doorway into the living room. She stops when she sees me. Lisa looks just like I knew she would. Different from me and my friends.

Her blond hair is cut short, and she must have three earrings in each ear. She's even wearing make-up. I wonder what my mom thinks of that!

And her clothes. None of my friends would ever wear an outfit like that. A baggy, ripped sweatshirt and paint-splattered jeans. Boys' hightops without laces.

Mom nudges me in the back. I know I'm supposed to say something. "Hi, Lisa. I hope you like it here."

Lisa nods slightly and takes a sip from her glass.

"Sarah, I told Lisa that you'd show her to her room and help her unpack."

"Sure," I say. I pick up Lisa's suitcase and carry it to the stairs. Lisa sets her glass on an end table and follows me. We go upstairs and down the hall to the guest room. Now it's Lisa's room.

"I'll just put your suitcase on the bed," I say.

"Okay," she mumbles.

I sit on the edge of the bed and watch Lisa as she opens her suitcase. She pulls out a stack of clothes and dumps them on the bed. I'm wondering if any of her clothes are all in one piece when I notice part of a book sticking out from a pile of clothes. The cover looks familiar. Not thinking, I reach over and pull the book out.

"Have you read that?"

Startled by Lisa's first complete sentence to me, I look up at her. "Are you kidding? This is my favorite book. I must have read it ten times!"

"Is that all?" Lisa sits down next to me. She takes the book from me and runs her fingers over the cover. "I just had to bring it with me. It's my favorite book, too," she says softly. "I'm surprised you like it."

"What do you mean?"

"Oh, you know. The way you are." Lisa seems to fumble for the words. "Your parents and your clothes and all." She turns back to her unpacking.

I scan my outfit. A pink sweater over a turtleneck, new jeans, and pink running shoes. Nothing wrong with my clothes. They're the same as my friends wear. They're different from what Lisa's used to, I guess.

Thinking about my clothes, I suddenly realize why Lisa hasn't smiled since I met her. I have to share my parents and my house, but she has to get used to everything being new and different. Including me. It must be harder on her than it is on me. And she knows less about me than I do about her. But I do know that we both like the book.

"Remember the part where the two girls get stuck in the cave?" I blurt out.

Lisa laughs. "And the part where the guy goes running down the hallway after them?"

We both laugh.

"Have you read any of her other books?" I ask Lisa.

"I didn't know she wrote any more."

"Oh, sure, lots. I have the whole series. Do you want to borrow them?" I ask her.

"If it's okay with you."

"It is." I jump up from the bed and head for my room. As I'm pulling books from the shelves and thinking how much we'll enjoy talking about them, something really nice occurs to me. Mom and Dad are getting a foster child, but maybe—just maybe—I'm getting a friend.

---

1. What would it be like for you to share your room, your parents, and your life with a stranger?

2. Can you tell by a person's face when they are ill at ease or unsure of themselves? Can you tell by body language?

3. Have you ever been in a situation where you were the only new person at a camp, school, or neighborhood?

Good-bye, Hospital—Hello, World

GOOD-BYE, HOSPITAL! I'm home at last.
My baby sister walks in hard-soled shoes now.
Marmalade, our cat, has had her kittens.
I have to share my brother with a girlfriend.
What happened to the grass beneath the swings?

So much is different now—have I changed, too?

HELLO, WORLD.

Marcella Fisher Anderson

Divided

We're not a unit anymore.
The family got divided.
I get two cakes,
but don't get too excited.

Two birthdays
can be kind of sad.
I'm learning to
subtract and add
faces to my party list.
Some are great
and others missed.

Birthdays didn't stop because
divorce divided up our hearts.
Now we party separately,
but get to multiply the parts.

Sara Holbrook

Here and There

I can't wait till I get there.
I really hate to leave.
Here I have my hamster,
there, my friend named Steve.

What will Mom be doing
while I'm not here to watch?
I'm nervous she'll be lonely
or sit and cry a lot.

I can't wait to see my daddy
and huggle in his chair.
Sometimes we buy pizza.
I have my own room there.

Mom says she won't be lonely
just 'cause she's alone.
Maybe I'll send a postcard
or call her on the phone.

My daddy says he needs me;
I brighten up his days.
We have to squeeze our sunshine
into weekend stays.

I think I have a headache
and I can't find my shoes.
It's time to go to Daddy's
and I've got transition blues.

Sara Holbrook

Moving

We are moving away
So I must say good-bye
To my room and my swing
And that sweet part of sky
That sometimes hangs blue
And sometimes hangs gray
Over the fields
Where I used to play.
Good-bye to my old friends
Jason and Sue
They wave from their porches,
Are they crying too?
The moving truck rumbles
Past all that I know—
The school and the woods
And the creek down below.
And everything seems
To be pleading
"Don't go!"

Eileen Spinelli

Loss Is Hard

Losing a loved one or experiencing any kind of separation is a hard emotion to deal with. Award-winning children's author Lois Lowry has written of her own experience while caring for her young granddaughter: ". . . I volunteerd to babysit so that [my daughter-in-law] Margret could have an evening with friends. It was not an easy decision for Margret. She had not left Nadine with a sitter for eleven months, not since the day. . . when my son, Nadine's Papa, had kissed them both good-bye, gone off cheerfully on a routine trip, and never returned. Nadine was too young to understand about plane crashes or death or why Papa never came back. . . ."

Although offered many diversions, the child was finally comforted and *reassured through story.* Her grandmother read and reread *Owl Babies* (Waddell), a picture book about four worried owlets whose mother has left the nest, but returns to cover her young with her protective wings.

Tire Swing Moments

By Virginia Kroll

When Noah was four, his much older brother, Seth, knew exactly what he needed. One day after school, Seth climbed the huge maple tree and attached it.

"A tire swing! A tire swing!" Noah cried, turning in circles.

"Just like the one I had when I was younger," Seth said. "Come on, I'll give you a push."

Seth pushed Noah until suppertime. Noah jumped off into Seth's long arms and hugged him as tightly as he could. "You're a nice man, Seth," he said.

Seth laughed. "Thanks, Little Brother."

Every day, Noah waited for Seth to come home from high school. Even on cold or rainy days, they shared some tire swing time before supper. Seth taught Noah how to push off and pump the swing by himself, and Noah started getting good at it.

One night after supper in late summertime, Seth told Noah that he was going away.

"Can you still come over for tire swing time?" Noah asked.

"I'm afraid not, Noah," Seth explained. "I'm

going to college far, far away. I'll be living there in a dorm. But I'll be home for vacations and summers."

Noah raced out of the house. He was angry with Seth. Mama came and found him. She hugged him and said, "I know you're upset. I'm a little sad that Seth is leaving, too. We'll miss him. But that's what people do when they grow up."

"Why?" Noah asked.

"Because it's time. Seth is a young adult now, Noah. He was already thirteen when you were born. I'm glad he wasn't any older than that or you two might never have gotten to know one another. And one year of tire swing moments is better than none at all, right?"

Noah thought about it for a second. "Right," he decided.

Two weeks later, Seth's friend Eric drove up in his car. He was going to college, too. He helped Seth pack his things. "Ready?" Eric asked when everything was finally squeezed in.

"Yeah," Seth said. Then he looked at Noah. "No. Wait a second, will you, Eric?"

Seth swung Noah up on his shoulders and carried him into the backyard. "How about one more super push?"

Noah swirled and twirled high in his tire swing, then he jumped into Seth's arms for a long good-bye hug.

Just before supper, Noah took his lonely feelings to the window. He stared into the backyard, remembering.

Mama said, "Why don't you go out and practice pumping on your swing? You're getting pretty good at it."

"No," said Noah. Then he thought about it for a second. "Yeah."

Noah ran into the backyard, thinking about Seth's first vacation. He climbed into the smooth black circle and let it hold him while he swayed. After all, he thought, a hug from Seth's tire swing was better than no hug at all.

---

1. Has someone special to you gone away?

2. Were you given something to remember him or her by?

3. How would you help a friend who felt sad and alone?

The Old Blue Rug

By Mary Elizabeth Miller

Matt awoke to a room full of sunshine. For a moment he forgot about Duchess, his dog who had died the day before as she lay on the old blue rug. That rug had been her bed for as long as Matt could remember. When he heard children playing in the field beyond the yard, he ran to the open window. "Shut up!" he yelled. How could they laugh and play as if nothing had happened? Didn't they know about Duchess? He banged the window shut and ran downstairs.

"Good morning, Matt." Mom had a treat of bright red strawberries that she poured over his cereal.

Matt's parents' voices were loud, and they laughed more than usual. When Matt spilled his orange juice, Mom just smiled and said, "No problem. These place mats are old, anyway."

He jumped from the table and ran into the living room. The old blue rug was gone. Duchess was gone.

Dad was right behind Matt. He took his hand and said, "Come with me, Matt. Help me bury her."

They carried the big dog's body wrapped in a blanket to the woods across the road. The tall grass was tangled and thick, but Dad soon cleared a place. When Mom crossed the road, they had just smoothed the dirt in the brown rectangle under a sycamore tree.

"I know that we will want to remember exactly where Duchess is, so let's put one of those big stones from the hillside here to mark the spot," Dad said. Together Mom, Dad, and Matt pushed a gray boulder onto the dirt.

After Dad and Mom went back across the road, Matt reached out and touched the big smooth stone with both hands. The day was warm, but Matt shivered. He stood a long time under the sycamore tree, then walked back to the house.

Saturday evening Aunt Janet and Uncle Bob came over to play cards. There was a big box in the back seat of their car. Matt peeked in. There lay a ball of white fur. The ball uncurled. Matt saw two pointed ears and a pink nose. Brown eyes looked up at him, and a fuzzy tail thumped against the box.

"What do you think of your new dog?" asked Uncle Bob.

"You keep him. I don't want him!" shouted Matt. He ran into the house past the grown-ups, who stood looking into the box.

Later, Matt sat in his rocking chair and watched TV, while Dad and Mom and Aunt Janet and Uncle Bob played cards. The puppy lay in the box and whined. The loud cries made Matt feel sad. He knew the dog missed its mother, but he pretended not to hear.

All the next week Mom fed the puppy. At mealtime it stood by the table looking up at Matt. Once it even pushed its bowl next to Matt's chair. Matt thought of Duchess and looked away.

Mom and Dad played with the puppy every evening after work. Matt played with the boy next door and remembered how well Duchess could catch a ball.

"The puppy is too big for his box now," Mom said one day. "I've washed Duchess's old blue rug. It's just perfect for the new dog. I'll put it in your room next to the bed."

Matt didn't say anything. When Mom wasn't looking, he folded the rug and put it on the top shelf of his closet.

That night he lay on his bed and looked out the window. A moon as red-gold as Duchess floated near a single star.

Matt tried not to, but he got up to look across the road. He saw the big stone under the sycamore tree. It looked cold and bare. The floor was cold and bare, too. He almost stepped on something warm and fuzzy. The little dog stirred and licked Matt's bare feet. For just a moment Matt stood, thinking, then went to the closet. Standing on tiptoe he reached for something on the top shelf. Stooping down, he picked up the puppy and gently laid it on the old blue rug.

---

1. Have you ever lost a pet: a goldfish, a cat, a hamster, a dog?

2. Did you do anything special to say good-bye?

3. How did you feel about replacing your pet with another one?

We

played
baseball
every spring.

He taught me
every single thing
I had
to know—

how to bat
to bunt
to throw.

But
since
he went away
that day
the game
will never
be the same.

The bleachers,
the bases,
the catcher's mitt
seem
empty

barren
now

like me

deserted
lonely
a
"Strike-three-
        OUT!"

And
I realize
what
losing
is
all
about.

Lee Bennett Hopkins

Remembering

My grandpa passed away last week
And I never knew before
That when a person dies,
You don't see him anymore.

Today I found our photo book.
That's me on Grandpa's knee.
We're laughing as he's reading
My favorite book to me.

And then I see us fishing
And waiting for a bite -
Bouncing in the choppy waves
Feeling lines go "tight."

Now here I am in winter
With Grandpa in a sleigh,
Skidding down a snowy slope.
What fun we had that day!
No reading, fishing, sledding now,
No chance to be together.
But pictures keep my grandpa living
In my mind forever.

Martha Thorpe

When Connie Died

When Connie died, I sat and cried.
Sadness lingered like a rainy day
whose steady dripping kept the chill inside.

At school, I didn't want to play.
No classmate there could take her place,
or be my partner for the race that May.

A new girl, Shirley, with a freckled face,
was someone many liked to tease.
She stood without a partner for the race.

I saw her face, which seemed so ill at ease,
I thought of Connie and knew what she would do.
Taking her hand, I gave a friendly squeeze.

She held my hand like Connie used to.
I knew to Connie I was being true,
and Shirley's smile, my way of breaking through.

Monica Gunning

Moving Day

Time to say a last good-bye
to all the things I know.
My yellow bedroom, empty now,
has a sad, secret glow.

My room, my yard, my maple tree
belong to another kid.
He'll climb the tree and run and swing—
do all the things I did.

Lisa Bahlinger

Respect—and Self-respect

An Orthodox Jewish boy with serious physical disabilities had been a foster child for several years until his foster parents could no longer give him a home. After lengthy inquiries, social workers found a new foster family eager to have him, but the family could not promise to keep a kosher kitchen. The boy wanted very much to be part of a family; but, rather than be untrue to a faith that had sustained him, he chose to live in an institution, where Judaic rites and traditions are observed.

This child was encouraged to read *The Always Prayer Shawl* (Oberman). The character, Adam, receives the prayer shawl from his grandfather, whom he loves and respects. In accepting the shawl, Adam realizes self-respect and an affirmation of his faith—an *emotional transfer* that supported the young reader in his decision.

Gabe the Great

By Barbara Briggs Ward

"Come on, Gabe! You can do it," my soccer teammates roared.

I couldn't believe it! The same kids who called me "Fat Boy" and "Lardo" in school were telling me I could do it!

The whistle blew. Coach had called time-out. Gathering the team around him, he said, "Okay, this is it. The last game of the play-offs. The last play in the shoot-out. We can go home with the trophy. Gabe, I want you to look him straight in the eyes. You can do it, son. I know you can."

All the guys—all my new buddies—gave me high-fives. "No one can get by you, Gabe," they told me.

That's what they used to say before this moment. Only then they were poking fun. My mother always told me that I was a "big-framed" boy. Every time I'd come home from school and tell her the names I'd been called, she'd say, "Someday, Gabe, these kids will realize what a great person you are. It's the size of the heart that matters—and you have a big heart, Gabe."

But that's not all that's big about me. The school doctor thought joining a sport might be good exercise for me. Some exercise! I warmed the bench all season. I wasn't fast enough to play the field. I couldn't dodge other players. "Here comes an earthquake," the guys would tease as I'd try to pass the soccer ball. So the coach decided to use me as a relief goalie. But he never needed to use me. What a relief!

Now, in the last game of the play-offs, we'd gone into overtime, tied 2-2. When no one scored in overtime, the referee ruled that the game would be decided by a shoot-out. Each team would get three shots—just one player against the goalie. Our team scored one goal. Then it was the other team's turn to kick.

It had been a brutal game. The rain had made the field very slippery. The other two goalies on our team were down with injuries, and I was the only one left. Somehow I had stopped the opponent's first two players in the shoot-out. Now it was down to one last player.

Everyone huddled on the sidelines. The misty rain turned into a downpour. The other team's last shooter sprinted onto the field. He was tall and skinny—really skinny! He was all knees and elbows, and I figured that if he took off his shirt every rib would show.

He ran around making practice kicks and cracking his gum. When the whistle blew, a cheer of "Go, Gabe, go!" rose over the jeers of "Fat Boy can't stop you!"

Clouds of rain drifted over the field. I blocked everyone out. It was just me and the skinny kid. I felt my "big heart" pounding under my drenched jersey. He tapped the ball back and forth with his left foot. Our eyes met. He smiled a crooked grin. I crouched into position, the elastic of my gym shorts cutting into my stomach. My legs felt like dead weight. The skinny kid stepped back several feet and then trotted toward the ball. As he pulled back to strike, my first instinct was to lunge to the right. But something inside told me no. I stood my ground. Suddenly he turned toward the left corner of the net. I heard a *smack* as his foot made contact with the ball. A spray of water came at me, along with a whirling soccer ball. My face was drenched; my eyes filled with rain.

I cleared my eyes. The ball was whizzing toward the highest corner. I leaped into the air, giving it all I had. I felt as if I were in flight! My fingertips, numb with cold, fumbled with the ball. Down I went, buried in mud. I heard the whistle.

"No goal," yelled the referee.

We won. *We won!* I had caught the ball! As I got to my feet, I was surrounded by teammates. "Gabe the Great!" they cheered. Somehow they lifted me on top of many sets of shoulders and carried me around the field.

As we made our way off the field, some of the guys began to make fun of the skinny kid who was slowly going back to the sidelines.

"Hey! Boney! Better get some meat on those bones! Go back home, Sticks!"

"Let me down, guys," I said.

The rain had stopped. I walked over to the skinny kid.

"Good shot," I said. "You gave it your best."

"Thanks," he said, and we shook hands. Suddenly the sun broke between the clouds, just like in a corny movie. I might never be a real soccer star, but at that moment, I felt great.

---

1. Have you ever shown respect for your opponent?

2. Did you find it hard to do?

3. Were you ever in a situation where your teammates thought you could not do a good job?

The Day of the Bamboo Horse

By Elizabeth Van Steenwyk

Chief Samurai. That's what Shigeo's friends would call him after today's secret game in the secret place. His friends would show him new respect after he led their team, the Sunlords, to victory over the dreaded Dragons and their captain, Kishi.

Shigeo stared at himself in the mirror above his desk as he tied the yellow band of the Sunlords over his straight black hair. He was taller than most boys in the sixth grade, with a look of determination in his eyes. The look of a samurai, he thought.

Ever since his class read about the warriors on stilts who saved Japan in a fierce battle, he had felt like one of them. Many centuries ago a foreign army came ashore in an invasion attempt, but they became mired down in swampy lowlands. Local farmers, who stood on stilts to plant the land, now put the stilts to another use. Fearlessly, they waded into the swamps and drove the invaders into the sea.

The story fired the imagination of Shigeo and the other boys in the sixth grade. They made stilts of the strongest bamboo. At first they played simple sports on them, such as team tag, but soon they searched for something more daring.

One day they invented the game and pledged themselves to secrecy. There was a feeling among them that their elders would not approve. And elders' wishes must be respected.

Shigeo hurried outside and picked up his stilts. Great-Uncle and his friends sat on a bench in a corner of the garden. They were old and wrinkled like fine parchment, talking softly of their long, long lives. One day Shigeo, too, would be talking with his friends about his life and his great defeat of Kishi.

Now Shigeo headed for the path and twisted his way among the bamboo trees. It was dense and dark in the thick woods, but he found the way easily. Soon he parted the sharp brambles that scratched at his pants legs and stepped into the secret clearing. Both teams, nine members each, were waiting.

"Hah, I thought you'd be too scared to come, Shigeo," Kishi's voice jeered. His eyes were glittery hard.

Shigeo ignored him. "I am ready," he said. "Take your places, Sunlords."

The teams walked to opposite ends of the clearing. The Sunlords checked their yellow headbands while the Dragons adjusted their green ones. It was the goal of the opposite team to remove the headbands any way they could. The first team to lose its headbands also lost the game.

"Mount up," Kishi shouted, and everyone hopped up on their stilts. They faced one another in the sudden, tense silence.

"Charge!" Shigeo cried. Both teams advanced. To Shigeo, the thudding of the stilts on the hard-packed ground sounded much like horses' hooves: bamboo horses of the true samurai.

Now both teams came together, shouting, pushing, and reaching for headbands. Kishi and his Dragons seemed especially fierce today. They charged forward again and again, rushing the Sunlords, barely giving them time to breathe. Shigeo saw three of his best players quickly lose their headbands and drop off to the sidelines.

Shigeo called for time-out after fifteen minutes, and the Sunlords gathered around him. Tenge, Shigeo's best friend, spoke up. "Kishi said he would not lose today. He will win no matter what he has to do."

Shigeo smiled. "And that is the way I feel, too," he said. "I will win no matter what." He thought of his plan and smiled even more.

Play resumed. The afternoon wore on, and one by one, players dropped out as they lost their headbands. Now only four boys remained on the field: Kishi and one from his team, and Shigeo and Tenge of the Sunlords.

Kishi advanced on Shigeo, but what had happened to the other Dragon? Shigeo heard someone behind him and tensed. He had let himself be trapped! Then he saw Tenge coming to help. Tenge charged the Dragon behind Shigeo, forced him out of position, and grabbed his green headband.

But Tenge had left himself defenseless. Kishi rushed Tenge and grabbed his headband. Now only the two captains remained.

Kishi moved forward. Shigeo began to back toward the edge of the clearing. Slowly, as if in a kind of dance, they moved, matching steps with each other. Shigeo licked his dry lips and felt sweat trickle down his face, but he never took his eyes from Kishi's.

Then he stopped, feeling the sharp brambles at the edge of the clearing brush against his legs. His plan was working. Kishi lunged for Shigeo's headband, but Shigeo was ready. Swiftly he sidestepped and watched as Kishi began to fall, face first, into the sharp brambles.

But in a flash of his mind's eye, Shigeo saw something else. He saw old men on a bench in a garden, not Great-Uncle and his friends, but himself and his own friends, in some future time. They would speak of Kishi and his terrible scars, and how it had happened in a secret game long before. And then they would look at Shigeo with accusing eyes because he had caused the scars just to win a game.

Shigeo grabbed Kishi, helping him get his balance just in time to step off his stilts and avoid falling into the brambles.

Kishi turned to look at Shigeo. "You won," he said. "You are the Chief Samurai."

"No." Shigeo interrupted the words that he once would have given anything to hear. "This isn't a sport anymore. Let's play something else."

Slowly, Kishi's eyes lost their hardness. "You're right, Shigeo," he said finally. "What do you think about baseball? We have enough players for two teams."

Shigeo nodded. They turned and walked slowly back to the village, together.

---

1. Could you call a halt to a dangerous activity?

2. Would you be afraid of what others might think of you for doing so?

3. How do you decide whether or not an activity is dangerous? Have you ever had to figure it out? Were you able to think straight?

Everybody's Hero

By Steve Garagiola

Little Man kicked angrily at the blacktop. The Packard Street Knights had scored their third straight basket, and their fans jumped up, howling and dancing to the driving beat of the music blaring across the basketball court.

The Knights led Little Man's team, the Fab Five, by three points. There was less than a minute to play in the YMCA summer league championship game.

"Time-out!" a voice called, and the referee blew his whistle, freezing the large red numbers of the clock at forty-two seconds.

"Come on, Little Man," Brian said as the Fab Five headed for the sidelines. "Keep your head in the game."

The Fab Five formed a tight circle around Brian, their captain, who yelled instructions over the noise of the crowd.

Little Man had brought this team together—he'd thought up the name, recruited the players, and had called all the plays at first. Though he stood a head shorter than anyone else on the court, Little Man had the speed and the talent to run with any of the older kids.

That was before Brian arrived.

"We don't need him," Little Man had said to Doughnut and Rudy. "He'll just hog the ball and ruin everything."

But Brian was too good to leave off the team. "Are you kidding?" Rudy had said. "Brian's great. We're a cinch to win with him."

So now "Mr. Perfect" called all the plays. Little Man's stepbrother, Brian, who never had time for Little Man off the court, would gladly step in and be the hero.

"Okay, Little Man," shouted Brian over the noise. "Work it inside to me or Rudy."

Little Man glared at Brian. "I know."

With the ball back in play, Little Man calmly dribbled to midcourt, his eyes darting between the scoreboard and his teammates. Brian streaked out from underneath the basket, fighting his way into the corner. "I'm open!" he yelled.

Little Man saw him, but froze when their eyes met. Sure, Brian, he thought, you be the hero. Don't let me get in your way.

In that instant of hesitation, Brian's man fought through the screen of bodies, and the clear passing lane disappeared. Little Man forced a dangerous pass to Rudy, who lofted a soft ten-foot shot off the backboard and through the net.

"Good hustle, Rudy!" Brian shouted.

Little Man knew he'd made a mistake, and he waited for his stepbrother to call him on it.

"Wake up!" Brian shouted, jabbing his finger toward Little Man. "Play some defense."

The words burned like acid.

Thirty-one seconds remained as the Knights crossed the half-court line. Number 14 dribbled smoothly to his left, shielding the ball with his body. He sneaked a quick glance at the clock, and Little Man seized the opportunity with a flick of his hand. The players scrambled for the loose ball, and Little Man grabbed it. He raced toward the basket with Number 14 at his heels.

"I'm on your right!" Brian yelled.

As Little Man neared the basket, he felt Number 14 closing in. But no way would he pass the ball. He wasn't giving away the game-winning basket. It was his turn to be a hero.

Little Man planted his foot and leaped, reaching toward the backboard for a lay-up. The ball floated toward the rim as if in slow motion. Little Man no longer saw his step-brother, or the crowd, or Number 14's long, thin arm stretching out from behind, knocking the ball away.

Swat! The action returned to normal speed as the ball sailed into the bleachers. The crowd roared.

"Little Man, Re-JECT-ed!" a voice yelled, and a group of older kids laughed, pointing their fingers in rhythm and chanting, "You! You! You!"

Little Man felt the heat rise in his face.

"Twenty-two seconds!" called Brian.

The referee handed the ball to Little Man, who searched for an open teammate to pass to.

The ball flew to Rudy, to Brian, to Doughnut, and with one bounce back to Little Man near center court.

The Knights suddenly broke into a new defensive scheme, hoping to confuse the Fab Five, who trailed by a single point with sixteen seconds left.

"Man to man!" Brian shouted.

"I know it, Brian!" Little Man snapped. He knew what the Knights were up to. They would have two players guard Brian to keep the ball away from him, daring Little Man to try to win it on his own. I'll show them all, he thought.

Number 45 stood in the way, flexed low, arms stretched out wide. He bounced lightly on his feet, challenging Little Man with a taunting grin. "Come on," he said. "Let's see what you've got."

Little Man dribbled with a steady rhythm that was nearly drowned out by the fans stomping their feet on the bleachers. I can beat this guy, he thought. I don't need Brian. I can win this game.

Little Man watched his teammates scrambling to get open. The final seconds of the game were ticking away.

Now! Little Man faked to the left with a flick of his shoulder and sensed his opponent fall slightly back on his heels. I've got you beat, Little Man thought as he drove hard to his right. The prize was an open path to the basket.

Seven, six, five—the seconds ticked down as Little Man drove, planted his foot, squared his shoulders to the basket, and jumped, stretching toward the rim. This time he saw the long arm reaching for the ball, but he knew it would arrive too late.

Even Little Man wasn't sure why he chose not to shoot. There was Brian, fighting through the two players guarding him in the corner, and Little Man zipped the ball toward him as Number 14 swiped at the air.

The ball slammed into Brian's chest, and he scrambled to grab it, tearing it away from a defender. Three, two, one—Brian released an off-balance shot that knuckled toward the basket and fell like a brick off the rim.

The final buzzer sounded. The Fab Five stood frozen on the court. They had lost.

By the time Little Man emerged from the locker room, only a few stragglers remained near the bleachers that had rumbled and shook thirty minutes earlier.

"What took you so long?" Brian asked.

"I didn't tell you to wait for me," Little Man snapped back.

"Just come on," Brian said. "I want to get home. I'm hungry."

"How can you be hungry after what happened?"

"Don't look at me, pal," Brian said, turning his back on Little Man. "I didn't give the game away. You did."

Brian pushed open the gate in the chain link fence. For three blocks they walked briskly in silence, Brian walking slightly ahead. Little Man focused on the path of a stone as he kicked it every fourth step. In front of the Polk Avenue playground, the stone slipped into a storm drain, and Brian broke the silence.

"I was open, and you wouldn't pass me the ball," he said. "Then in the last second I'm double-teamed and you pass up a perfect shot to force a dumb pass to me. Why didn't you shoot?"

Little Man stopped walking and braced himself for a fight. He'd been waiting for that question.

"Hey, I made a mistake," he said. "Get off my back."

Brian turned to face Little Man. "Not good enough, little brother. I want to know why you did that."

"Because I thought I might miss," Little Man said.

"That's a lousy reason."

Little Man pawed at the sidewalk with the toe of his worn sneaker, then looked squarely at Brian. "I wanted *you* to miss."

Brian had no answer. He shook his head slightly. "That's a worse reason," he said quietly, then leaned against the fence.

Little Man stood firm as he and Brian eyed each other like strangers on the first day of school. Finally Brian spoke. "So you must have been happy when I bricked that shot and we lost."

Little Man looked down at the storm drain that had swallowed his rock. His eyes began to fill, and he blinked hard. "No," he said quietly. "I felt lousy. I let the team down."

"You let yourself down," Brian said, turning to walk away. Then he turned back. "Besides—you're good. You would have made that shot."

Little Man stared at the ground a moment, then looked up as his mouth curled into a slight smile. "You think so?"

Brian jammed his hand into his pocket where he had stuffed a five-dollar bill that morning. "You want to go get a hamburger or something?"

"Sure," Little Man answered. "I'm starving."

---

1. Have you ever felt overshadowed by another's greater talent?

2. Have you been surprised to learn that other people think highly of you?

3. Is there anything you think you are good at? Do you enjoy the activity even though others might also be good at it—or perhaps better?

The New Kid

Our baseball team never did very much,
we had me and PeeWee and Earl and Dutch.
And the Oak Street Tigers always got beat
until the new kid moved in on our street.

The kid moved in with a mitt and a bat
and an official New York Yankees hat.
The new kid plays shortstop or second base
and can outrun us all in any race.

The kid never muffs a grounder or fly
no matter how hard it's hit or how high.
And the new kid always acts quite polite,
never yelling or spitting or starting a fight.

We were playing the league champs just last week;
they were trying to break our winning streak.
In the last inning the score was one-one,
when the new kid swung and hit a home run.

A few of the kids and their parents say
they don't believe that the new kid should play.
But she's good as me, Dutch, PeeWee, or Earl,
so we don't care that the new kid's a girl

Mike Makley

ME I AM!

I am the only ME I AM
who qualifies as me;
no ME I AM has been before,
and none will ever be.

No other ME I AM can feel
the feelings I've within;
no other ME I AM can fit
precisely in my skin.

There is no other ME I AM
who thinks the thoughts I do;
the world contains one ME I AM,
there is no room for two.

I am the only ME I AM
this earth shall ever see;
that ME I AM I always am
is no one else but ME!

Jack Prelutsky

Don't Worry if Your Job Is Small

Don't worry if your job is small,
And your rewards are few.
Remember that the mighty oak,
Was once a nut like you.

Anonymous

Alone—
and Sometimes Lonely

A teacher in a Wisconsin school said that she reads *Fly Away Home* (Bunting) to her class in preparation for the expected arrival of a child from the local shelter. The story is about Andrew, a homeless boy who lives at the airport with his unemployed father. Each day, Andrew watches a sparrow fly freely in and out of the open doors, returning each evening to its airport home.

This book *heightens sensitivities* among the classroom children as they identify with the character's sense of loneliness in his uprooted circumstances.

Joey and the
Fourth-of-July Duck

By Diane Burns

Ba-*Boom!* Glittery red and silver gashes split the night sky. Joey snuggled, stomach down, on the city pier and studied the fireworks' reflection in the lagoon beneath him.

"Oooohh," breathed everyone crowded along the shore.

Joey wondered if the sky minded being blown apart. Maybe not, because whenever colors ripped the blackness, the night quickly mended itself. Well, he couldn't ask Lonnie about it. Joey's words never came out fast enough to suit his big brother.

Lonnie talked fast, he walked fast, he even ate fast. And though Lonnie shared his secrets and his fishing tackle with his little brother, he sometimes called Joey "Slow-Joe," the way the townsfolk did.

Ba-Boom! Green puffballs somersaulted high into the air. Their creamy smoke trails came sliding down.

"It's a mirror picture," Joey said, watching the water. "A beautiful mirror picture." He looked around, but no one was laughing at him. In fact, no one had heard him at all. His perch on the pier had taken him beyond anyone's teasing.

"Slow isn't a bad thing." Joey spoke to the smooth, dark water. "Teacher says slow helps me draw better pictures."

Fireworks burst overhead like popcorn. They reminded him of a leftover snack in his pocket. But as he felt for it, *BA-BOOM!*

Everyone jumped at the extra loud noise. A ripple splashed out from under the pier, spoiling Joey's mirror picture. Something in the water had been surprised by the loud noise, too. Some afraid-thing splashed and then fluttered under the pier. Joey peeked between the slats.

Beneath him, water lapped like melted chocolate against a tangle of arrow-shaped reeds. A shivering duck shape huddled there.

At another *BOOM!* Joey heard her soft, terrified *quaarck!* She paddled back and forth, back and forth, a tiny prisoner trapped by people and noise. Her honest eye studied Joey.

She wants me to help her, Joey thought, but I don't know how. "Stay here, Duck. It's safe," he said. "The noise will go away pretty soon."

Joey remembered the popcorn in his pocket and pulled out a mashed handful. He was hungry for a snack. Maybe Duck was, too. Joey dropped one stale piece of popcorn. It touched Duck's sleek head and bounced onto the water beneath her bill. Joey smiled. He was treating Duck to tasty fireworks from the sky.

"One for you," he said. He crunched a half-popped kernel in his teeth. "And one for me."

Duck bobbed up and down like a cork, holding her place in the reeds. She watched as Joey kept half of the popcorn for himself and dropped the rest onto the water. Joey watched as Duck arched her neck toward a floating white tidbit and swallowed it.

"Chew slow. The taste lasts longer," Joey said.

"*Quaack,*" agreed Duck.

With the last of the fireworks booming like drum thunder in their ears, Joey and the duck enjoyed their snack together. Then all was quiet, except for sounds of bump and bustle that meant everyone was heading home. The fireworks were over for another year.

Two quick steps rattled the pier. Joey knew without looking that Lonnie had found him.

"I have to go home now," Joey whispered.

But the Fourth-of-July duck was too busy with the last of her treats to hear him.

Joey pulled himself to his feet, carefully so he wouldn't scare Duck. He murmured, "Lonnie, have you got any popcorn left?"

"Part of a box." Lonnie's quick voice slowed a little. "Are you hungry, Joey? Here."

Lonnie thrust the paper box toward his brother. Joey reached for it, but the box tipped. Popcorn spilled onto the pier.

Lonnie turned away. "Slow-Joe," he sighed. "Come on."

Joey pushed the spilled popcorn down between the cracks of the pier. "A Slow-Joe is an okay thing," he whispered to the duck shape still nodding among the reeds. Duck nosed forward toward the newly fallen treats.

"Come on, Joey. Let's go home." Lonnie's voice came impatiently, faintly, through the dark. "The popcorn's wasted, anyhow."

Joey didn't like to hurry, but sometimes it couldn't be helped. And he knew the popcorn wasn't wasted. Not really. But Lonnie wouldn't understand.

Joey would come back in the morning. Duck might still be under the pier. She had taken her time with the popcorn snack, so she might not hurry away.

But even if Duck went away before the morning, it wouldn't matter. "I'll remember you," Joey whispered to the Fourth-of-July duck. He turned and stepped from the pier to the land, following his big brother.

---

1. Do you know someone who is slow to understand things? In what ways could you be a friend to that person?

2. What are that person's special qualities?

3. If someone like Joey were your brother, how would you feel about him?

Camp Songs

By Geanie M. Roake

Ellie's mother looked worried. "Are you sure you're going to be okay?" she asked.

"Yes, Mom," Ellie said, giving her mother a quick hug. "Please don't cry."

"All aboard for Round Lake Camp," called the driver.

"I've got to go, Mom. I promise I'll have a great time."

That's what Ellie said, but she didn't believe it. She knew this would be the longest week of her life. The old yellow bus chugged into motion and the parents in the churchyard waved their last good-byes. Ellie envied them. She wished she were going home. But here she was, on her way to Round Lake Camp for an eternity of seven whole days.

Mom and Dad had said that Ellie spent too much time alone and that a week at camp would be just the thing. Ellie couldn't agree less. She liked being alone.

Ellie loved their farm and the frog pond and her long country rambles with Moses, her big black dog. She didn't have many friends. Friends were hard to come by, and they never seemed to find Ellie. She didn't see why it would be any different at camp.

Ellie and the others received a rousing camp welcome of songs and cheers, then were marched off to their cabins by the counselors. The path ran along a lake that looked cool and inviting on this hot, sticky day.

"Bet there are fish in there as long as my arm," Ellie thought. Back home she had a secret hideout near her fishing hole. It was cool and shady and quiet as a whisper.

The sun beat down and dust rose from the trail as the noisy group scuffled along. Soon they reached a fork in the path. The boys went one way, the girls the other toward their cabins.

The cabins were arranged in a circle by the campfire ring. Ellie found her bunk in Maple Cabin and looked around. The room was already bursting with girls—girls shrieking with laughter, chattering back and forth, and bouncing off the beds. How could these kids already know each other?

Ellie tried to make herself as small as possible, but she hoped someone would talk to her and include her in the group. No one did.

"Oh, well." She sighed. She was used to this. But it was one thing to be alone at home, and quite another to be alone among all these kids.

That first day seemed to drag on forever. The campers bustled from one activity to another: in and out of the cookhouse for meals, into the roundhouse for arts and crafts, back to the cabin for skits and singing.

That night Ellie couldn't sleep. Her counselor snored, and Ellie had to get up three times to go to the bathroom. At least she had a bunk by the window. The stars sparkled and danced like spider webs on a dewy summer morning, and Ellie could hear crickets and frogs in the distance. She pretended she was camping in her own backyard, and after a while she drifted off to sleep.

By the second night Ellie felt lower than a lizard's tail. She felt as if she'd been at camp for two weeks instead of two days.

As she lay listening to the night sounds, Ellie heard a new song. She looked out the window and saw Terra, a counselor from the Sycamore Cabin. She was sitting by the fire with her guitar.

Terra sang beautiful songs, softly so as not to disturb anyone. The songs seemed to match Ellie's mood. There was one about a shepherdess who walked and walked, looking for a lost sheep, and another about a sailor away at sea.

Suddenly Ellie couldn't stand to be lonesome in the dark cabin any longer. She slid off her bunk and hurried outside in her bare feet. Terra looked up in surprise, than patted the space on the log next to her.

"Can't sleep?" she asked.

Ellie shook her head and sat down. "Those were pretty songs," she said.

Terra strummed the guitar for a moment. "Your name's Ellie, right?"

Ellie nodded her head, surprised that Terra would remember.

"Is this your first time away from home?"

Ellie nodded again.

"Well," Terra said, "how do you like it so far?"

Ellie was determined not to be a baby. She started to say "Great," but she choked on the word. Her eyes began to tear. She told Terra how homesick she was.

Terra patted Ellie's arm. "You know what I do when I'm feeling lonely?" she said. "I look for someone else who's feeling the same way, and I go and talk to her. Chances are, she needs a friend as much as I do."

That had never occurred to Ellie. She thought you just waited for friends to come to you.

The next day started with a four-mile hike.

"Everybody find a partner," shouted the head counselor.

Ellie looked at the ground. Then she remembered Terra's advice. She raised her eyes and looked around. There was a girl off to the side of the path, looking as miserable as Ellie had been feeling. She walked slowly toward the girl.

"Hi," she said. "I'm Ellie. Want to be my partner?"

The girl looked up in amazement. Then her face lit up like the sun. "Sure!" she said.

Ellie smiled, and her spirits soared. Maybe friends weren't so hard to come by after all.

---

1. Do you think Ellie was the only one at camp who felt conspicuous and lonely? Did the other campers just cover up their feelings of not belonging?

2. Why did Ellie forget about feeling lonely when she asked the other girl to be her hiking partner?

3. What kinds of things do you do when you are feeling lonely?

Window Cat

Cat upon the window sill,
Window Cat,
What is it that you're seeing,
that you stare intently at?

Do you see a yellow bird,
a purple butterfly?
Or do you dream of tasty snacks—
some goldfish swimming by?

Window Cat, I'm just like you—
wishing I were elsewhere, too.

Donna E. Peltz

Alone in My Hospital Room

I built some magic towers
During my hospital stay.
I didn't want to leave my room—
to paint, to paste, to play.
I built the towers higher,
Higher, where the treetops sway.
They guarded me all through the night.

At dawn they went away . . .

Marcella Fisher Anderson

Alone

I am alone . . . and lonely.

My own sadness makes everything around me
  more beautiful.
The dusk falls softly,
As simply as a page turning or a bird lighting on the ground.
The sky grows dull rose near the rooftops
And, high above me, a sea-blue-green.
I am caught up in it all—and small.
I search for words. I ache with words I cannot find.

Inside, the phone rings.
"Where's Kate?" Dad asks.

I am here—but I say nothing.
He calls—but I do not answer.

"She's not in yet," he says to someone.
"I'll tell her you phoned."

I could go in.

Soon it will be suppertime anyway,
Time for eating and talking and being part of things,
Belonging again to the horrible, boring, nice, funny,
  noisy, busy, angry, loving world of people.

I'll go in when I have to.
In half an hour, I'll even like it.

Now . . .
Now I'll stay out here, hugging my separateness,
  my oneness

I am alone. I am lonely.
I am growing into me.

Jean Little

Alone

Alone
doesn't have to be sad
like a lost-in-the-city dog.

Alone
doesn't have to be scary
like a vampire swirled in fog.

Alone
can be slices of quiet,
salami in between
a month of pushy hallways
and nights too tired to dream.

Alone
doesn't have to be
a scrimmage game with grief.
Alone
doesn't have to argue,
make excuses or compete.
Like having nothing due,
sometimes.
Alone
is a relief.

Sara Holbrook

41

One Day at a Time

A twelve-year-old boy with a slowly progressing neurological disease returned frequently to the hospital. Each time, he borrowed *St. George and the Dragon* (Hodges) from the hospital library. As he *identified with the main character*, the child "became" St. George, the young, untested knight who finally slays the dragon, saves the kingdom from total desolation, and marries the king's beautiful daughter. Perhaps during each reading, the young boy carried the bright shield of St. George and swung his shining sword against a mystifying illness—raising his own struggle to the mythic plane found in the story.

JUST LIKE BEING THERE

By Elizabeth Weiss Vollstadt

"**N**othing could be worse than having this disease. Nothing," Amanda said to her twin sister, Amy. Tears filled her hazel eyes as she lay in the hospital bed.

Her cheerleader uniform was draped over the room's only chair. The afternoon sun shone on the red and white skirt, the crisp white blouse, and the oversized red sweater with a big *D* for Delaney Junior High.

But was she getting ready to put it on and cheer at the championship basketball game? No. Once again, cystic fibrosis had taken over her life and sent her to the pediatric hospital. Why me? she thought for the millionth time. Why me?

Her brother, Michael, wasn't sick. Even Amy—whose brown eyes and dark hair made it clear that they weren't identical twins—was healthy. Only she had inherited the two genes that gave her cystic fibrosis.

Amanda knew all about cystic fibrosis. It was why she sometimes struggled to breathe, why she coughed a lot, and why a simple cold could send her to the hospital. Usually she could handle it. But not now. Not today. Not when Amy was standing there in her own uniform.

"Hey, Amanda, I gotta go," said Amy. "Dad's waiting downstairs. See you after the game, okay?"

"Right," answered Amanda, looking out the window instead of at her sister.

Amy hopped off Amanda's bed. "I'm really sorry you can't come," said Amy. "But I'll tell you about the game—basket by basket." She touched Amanda's shoulder. "And we'll do a special cheer, just for you."

"A lot of good that'll do," snapped Amanda, turning to glare at her sister.

The smile left Amy's face. "I'm really sorry," she said again.

"Yeah, well I am, too," Amanda answered. "More than *you'll* ever know." She turned back toward the window.

Amy said nothing else. Her steps were slow as she left the room.

For a moment Amanda felt guilty about making her sister feel bad. "Wait," she almost called out. But she didn't. It just wasn't fair that Amy could do everything—everything—and she couldn't.

The afternoon dragged. Amanda kept looking at the clock on the wall. She could picture the toss to start the game . . . hear the crowd roar when the first basket was scored . . . and feel the thrill of chanting, "We want a basket . . . over there!"

Only she wasn't there. She was here, with an IV in her arm, watching the slow drip of the antibiotics through the clear plastic tube.

The sky was bright orange from the setting sun when Amy came running into Amanda's room. Six other girls rushed in behind her, still wearing their red and white cheerleader uniforms. They crowded around Amanda's bed.

"Quick, Amanda," said Amy, "put on your uniform. The game's about to start."

"What do you mean? It's all over. Who won?" Amanda asked. She looked at Dena, another cheerleader.

Dena grinned. "You'll have to watch like everyone else."

Amy held up a tape. "It's all here. We thought we'd watch it with you. We can all cheer together. Get your uniform on!"

"I can't. I'm all hooked up." Amanda held up her arm with the IV.

"Oh yes you can," said a nurse, who had followed the girls into the room. She took the IV bag from the pole. "I'll cap the flow for a minute while you get changed."

"This is stupid," Amanda muttered. But the nurse was hurrying her out of bed and into the bathroom. When they came out, Amanda was dressed in her uniform. The nurse led her to the activity room. Amy started the VCR that she had hooked up to the room's television.

Delany's team, the red one, got the ball first. Down to the basket raced David, a ninth grader. A leap—basket! The crowd on the videotape roared. The cheerleaders in the activity room yelled.

Amanda folded her arms.

The game went on. Amy, Dena, and the other cheerleaders yelled when the red team scored and groaned when the white team took the lead. Only Amanda said nothing.

Then it was time-out. The cheering squad on the tape raced onto the floor.

"Come on, Amanda, let's cheer," pleaded Amy.

"No, this is stu . . ." Amanda began.

"It is not!" Dena grabbed Amanda's free arm. "Do you think it's easy for Amy—and us—to see you miss out on things? Or do you just like feeling sorry for yourself?"

She pulled Amanda out of the chair she was sitting in. They joined the other cheerleaders lined up near the window.

"Okay," yelled the cheerleader captain. "Let's go! Who we gonna cheer for? Delaney, Delaney."

Amanda stood still when the other girls started to cheer. Was Dena right? Did she like feeling sorry for herself? Amy and the other girls were reliving the game—just for her. It wouldn't change anything, but maybe she could at least try to have fun.

So Amanda stepped right, then left, bent down, jumped up. "Delaney, Delaney, let's go!" she yelled.

Now it was the second half. Amanda started watching the game. Soon she cheered with her friends when their team pulled ahead again. She yelled, "Defense!" when the other team scored. She almost forgot she was in the hospital when Carlos grabbed a rebound to make a basket. And each time there was a time-out, she got up to cheer.

Finally the game was over. Delaney had won, 67-58.

"What a great game!" Amanda said, surprised that she really meant it. She looked at her friends huddled around her chair. A crowd of nurses and other patients had gathered in the doorway to watch and clap. They smiled at her.

"I guess there could be something worse than having CF," she said finally. "It would be having CF and *not* having such great friends!"

Her eyes met Amy's. "And a great sister!" She squeezed Amy's hand. "I'm sorry I was such a jerk before. What a great idea to tape the game. It was just like being there."

Amy smiled. "Hey, what are sisters for? Now get well quickly so you can come home."

"I will," Amanda said, "just as fast as I can."

---

1. Have you ever been disappointed by a change in plans?

2. Describe a time when you were able to turn a disappointment into a positive event.

3. If you knew someone with a chronic medical condition, how could you be a friend to that person?

Eye Trouble
or A Close Encounter of the Nutty Kind

By Victoria Smith Peters

My bus pulled up at school, and I peeked out the window—hoping. Rats! No luck. There he was. Jake Carter, also known as Jake the Terrible, Jake the Tormentor, Jake the Meanest Boy in Town.

Jake stuffed something into his backpack and grinned wickedly. I knew what he was up to. Jake Carter was waiting for *me*.

Every day Jake made me miserable. Each time I stepped out of the classroom, he was right around the corner, waiting to pounce.

Jake did awful things like calling me names and telling Mike Barr I wanted to marry him. Why did he pick on me? I had no idea.

Determined to ignore him, I rushed down the bus steps, my nose in the air. Jake stuck out his big foot and tripped me. Papers, books, and clarinet flew in every direction.

"You fell for it," Jake hee-hawed while I scrambled to pick it all up. "I can't believe you

didn't see me. What's the matter, Becky? You need glasses?"

Shooting him a dirty look, I jumped to my feet and raced away. I took deep breaths, trying not to shake. Jake had guessed my deepest, darkest secret. I needed glasses. The last person in the universe I wanted to know about my eye trouble was Jake Carter.

"What's wrong, Becky?" asked my friend Monica when I reached math class.

"Jake Carter as usual. He guessed that I need glasses. He was just joking, but what if he finds out it's true?" Six months ago I got glasses. Monica was the only person who knew about them besides my parents. Each morning I took them off the minute I left the house.

"It would be for the best. Really, Becky, you ought to wear them."

"Oh, no. It's bad enough having Jake call me Pinocchio Nose and Slime Face when I know it's not true. I couldn't bear it if he knew about the glasses."

"But you bump into things," Monica reminded me. "And . . . your grades are slipping." She pointed to the paper Mr. Hall was putting on my desk.

"Oh, no," I groaned, squinting at the large red *D* at the top of the test. "What did I do wrong?"

Monica compared our papers. "You misread numbers in five problems. Come on, Becky!" she cheered. "Put-On-Those-Glasses!" Since Monica has become a cheerleader, she breaks into chants at the weirdest times.

"Shhh! I'd rather flunk," I hissed.

Surely the day would get better. It couldn't get worse. But I was wrong. Jake was in rare form. He swiped my English book and hid it in the boys' locker room. At lunch he dumped a shaker of pepper on my food when my back was turned. Unfortunately, I didn't see the pepper, and I took a big bite. My eyes watered for an hour.

Revenge was sweet. Jake was running for the bus when I grabbed his backpack and dumped everything on the ground. He turned bright red as if he was embarrassed. Best of all, Jake walked home. I wish I could have seen his expression as the bus pulled away without him. Ha, ha!

That evening something happened to change my mind about wearing glasses . . . the most terrifying event of my life!

I was on my way home from the store. It was getting dark, so I quickly put the milk and eggs in the basket of my bike and jumped on.

Two blocks from home a large, foreign object suddenly appeared in the sky. It hovered closely, its strange lights flashing on and off. I blinked. Surely my eyes were playing tricks on me!

A UFO. And it was coming after me! I crashed into a fire hydrant. Slowly, slowly the UFO closed in. I would never see my parents again!

"Good-bye, Mom and Dad. Good-bye, Monica. Be a good dog, Fluffy."

I would never see Jake again! Oh, well, every cloud has a silver lining.

Closer and closer the UFO crept. Any second a beam of light would vaporize me up into the alien spaceship. Suddenly, the bright lights flashed on again. BUY HARDY HARDWARE . . . THE BEST NUTS AND BOLTS IN TOWN . . .

It was a blimp!

"I'm the biggest nut in town," I muttered. My heart was pounding. I got up and surveyed the damage.

Broken eggs and milk coated the hydrant, my bike, and me. The wheel on my bike was bent. I had torn my new jeans and skinned my knee.

The next morning I put on my glasses and left them on.

When Jake saw me, he stopped dead in his tracks. His mouth was hanging open, and his eyes were about to pop.

I braced myself for the stream of cruel jokes. To my surprise, Jake turned his back to me and fumbled around in his backpack. When he turned around again, it was my turn to stare. Jake Carter was wearing glasses!

"I won't laugh if you don't," Jake said, grinning.

"You've got a deal." Then we both laughed.

Jake and I walked into school, talking—a normal, friendly conversation.

We *are* friends now. And I think that may have been what Jake wanted all along.

---

1. Have you ever felt self-conscious about wearing braces or glasses?

2. Has it helped to talk about it?

3. Why do some people tease others? Is it right to put someone down to build yourself up?

Playing by the Rules

By Molly A. Perry

"Hop . . . Hop . . . Hop," said Sarah to herself. "Three hops on one foot, then you hop on two feet," the girls in her first-grade class told her over and over. "If you want to play hopscotch you have to hop on one foot. That has always been the rule."

"I hate that rule," she said. "But I still want to play."

Sarah sat on the front porch steps. She watched Dad raking up the red and yellow leaves that decorated the front lawn.

Mrs. Rosen, who lived next door, opened her front door.

"Isaac!" she called to Dad. "Isaac, I need three eggs for my challah! Do you have any?"

"Yes, we do," Dad called back. "I'll ask Sarah to bring them over. You can't start the New Year without your beautiful round, raisin challah!"

"Good, she can help me knead the dough," said Mrs. Rosen. Her round face was pink from the heat in her kitchen.

Sarah grabbed the banister to help herself stand up, then walked down the porch steps. With each careful step she looked down at the white plastic braces on her legs. They went from her feet to right under her knees. "I'll think of a way to play. I've just got to," she said to herself.

"There she is!" said Dad when Sarah got to the bottom porch step.

Sarah swayed a little from side to side as she walked to her father. Her dark hair bounced around lightly as she picked up speed. Like a moth flying up to a porch light, Sarah ran right to Dad. Her arms went around him for a hug.

"I'll bring Mrs. Rosen the eggs," said Sarah, her cheek against Dad's soft, red flannel shirt. "I'll even help with the dough."

"What's this?" said Dad, looking at the tears in her eyes.

"Everyone at school is playing hopscotch," said Sarah. "I want to play."

"You'll have your eggs and your helper in a few minutes," called Dad to Mrs. Rosen.

Dad took Sarah's hand and walked with her to the wooden porch steps. They sat down together on the bottom step.

"Tell me what happened, Sarah," said Dad.

"One of the girls drew a hopscotch on the playground at school today. She showed everyone how to play. The rule is that you have to hop on one foot."

Sarah wiped her tears on the sleeve of her Cleveland Indians sweatshirt.

"Did you tell Mrs. Simon?" asked Dad. "She could help with the rules."

"No," said Sarah. "I want to play by the real rules."

"Okay," said Dad. "But how are you going to do that?"

"I don't know," said Sarah. She stomped up the porch steps to get the eggs. "Let me think about it." Having spina bifida makes it so hard to hop, she thought. She let the screen door slam behind her.

Sarah went into the kitchen. She smelled chicken soup cooking. The house smelled like "holiday." Soon Sarah would help Mom light the candles to begin the New Year. Sarah picked up one foot so she could hop on the other. Down she went. But she got up right away. This time she held on to the back of a kitchen chair. She picked up one foot. She let go of the chair. Sarah counted one . . . two . . . three . . . before she toppled to the floor. She got up again to give it another try. This time she held on to the back of the chair, lifted her foot, and hopped two times holding on!

"Sarah!" called her father. "Today, with the eggs!"

Sarah took three eggs out of the refrigerator, put them in a small basket, and took them to Mrs. Rosen's house.

For two weeks Sarah never walked in the house. She only hopped. She hopped along the walls, around the dining room table, holding on to the chair in front of the TV. Now and then she would let go and take a hop without holding on. One . . . two . . . and down she would go!

"Are you okay?" asked Mom once when Sarah toppled to the floor.

"I'm okay," said Sarah. "I just can't get past two hops."

"Let me call Mrs. Simon," said Mom. "You're going to be black and blue from falling all the time."

"No! Not yet," said Sarah. "Please, not yet!"

A week later Mrs. Simon said, "Let's take our recess outside. It's so beautiful out."

In no time the hopscotch was drawn on the sidewalk. This time Sarah got in line with the other girls.

Silently, everyone gathered around to see Sarah play hopscotch.

Sarah stuck her arms out like a bird, took a deep breath, and took one hop. She didn't fall. She took another hop and wobbled a little. Her heart went thump, thump, thump, but she did not fall. She closed her eyes tight and took another hop. She didn't fall down! Finally she landed on the double space, which took two feet. Hop . . . Hop . . . Hop . . . Sarah finished the hopscotch.

Everyone started to clap. Mrs. Simon came over to give her a hug.

"Come over after school today and play hopscotch," said one of the girls.

"Maybe tomorrow," said Sarah with a big smile. "Today, I'm helping Mrs. Rosen. We're going to make honeycakes. Mrs. Rosen says they help make the New Year sweet."

Sarah hopped two times. "It's a sweet year already!"

---

1. Do you know anyone who is left out of activities because of a disability? What could you do to help that child join in?

2. Tell about your own proudest accomplishment, and try to recall the steps you took to reach your goal.

3. Share an example of someone who is physically challenged who can still do things, i.e. a sight-impaired child who can ride a horse.

Bad Joke

Glasses and braces?
Is this some bad joke?
A conspiracy
so I look like a dope?
Plastic bug eyes
and tinsel buckteeth.
What'd I do to
deserve this grief?

Why can't I feel normal?
Why can't I feel good?
I'm hopeless and helpless
and misunderstood.
I can't stand this age,
and it's just my luck . . .
I'll turn out to be bald
when I finally grow up.

Sara Holbrook

Good-bye

I may have to come back to the hospital,
But I'm leaving for now. Good-bye!

While I'm out, I'm going to laugh at a duck,
And squint at the sun and the sky,

Smile more at my parents, tell them I love them,
Surprise them with all I can give.

While I'm out, I want to bust loose with my friends,
Bake cookies, eat pizzas—and LIVE.

I think I'll change my bedroom around,
Then lie out in the sun and fry.
I may have to come back to the hospital,
But I'm leaving for now. Good-bye!

Marcella Fisher Anderson

First Things First

Grandma hates my loud music,
Drive-in restaurants,
And not getting to bed before
The late news has begun.
She likes yucky green salads,
Pulling weeds,
Putting things away,
And getting up before the sun.
Mama says when I grow up
I may be more like Grandma,
But first things first,
I just dug a worm,
And I'm going fishing with Grandpa.

David Harrison

You Can Do It

An early childhood teacher in a pediatric setting read *The Little Engine That Could* (Piper) to a five-year-old boy who was struggling to regain mobility. Later in the day, the boy came down the hallway with his physical therapist. As he passed his teacher's open door, she heard him saying, "I think I can. I think I can," from the text of the book.

The boy had made a direct connection to a story recently read aloud. *The book gave the young child the words to put his efforts into focus.*

Riding the Wind

By Regina Hanson

Meg rolled her wheelchair along the docks, watching sailboats glide across the lake. Never again, she thought, could she ride the wind on a boat. Sadness wrapped itself around her chest, tight as a hungry boa constrictor.

"Going for a sail?" someone called.

Meg turned. On a boat docked nearby, a boy unfurled a sail. She recognized him—it was Jeff Anderson from school.

"I only came to watch," she mumbled. "I used to take sailing lessons—before my accident."

"Hey, Dad!" Jeff stuck his head into the boat's cabin. "Can Meg sail with us this afternoon?"

"I can't," Meg called. Her face felt hot. "My legs don't work."

Meg's parents came up behind her just as a man came out of the boat's cabin. "Why, hello, Tom," said the man, smiling.

"Mr. Anderson and I know each other from the office," explained Meg's father.

Mr. Anderson leaned over and shook Meg's hand. "You're all welcome aboard," he said.

"My dad has a master's license from the Coast Guard," said Jeff. "You're safe with us on *Dancer.*"

"Thanks for the invitation," said Meg's mother, "but our daughter's the only sailor in our family."

Her father added, "If Meg would like to sail, we'll gladly watch from shore."

The thought of sailing on *Dancer* made Meg's heart pound. She clenched her fists, angry at her useless legs. Fighting the pressure around her chest, she said bravely, "I'll go."

"Neat!" said Jeff. He helped as Meg's parents lifted her from the wheelchair into the boat.

The lake seemed darker now. Shuddering, Meg imagined it swallowing her. She put on a life jacket and hid her nervousness as the boat left the dock and her parents.

Jeff's dad sat opposite her in the cockpit, steering *Dancer* with the tiller. He handed her a rope attached to the larger of two sails. "You'll work the mainsail with this line, Meg. Jeff will handle both lines that control the jib."

Meg's hands trembled as she held her line. "I haven't done this since last summer."

"Sailing's like bicycling," said Jeff. "You never forget how."

Except, Meg thought, I bicycle only in my dreams now. The snake coiled around her chest again, squeezing, as it did whenever she fought tears.

Suddenly the mainsail started to flutter. Without thinking, Meg loosened her line, letting out the sail. The fluttering worsened.

"Sorry." Embarrassed, Meg pulled in the sail so

it caught wind at a better angle. *Dancer* heeled, skimming the water like a great white bird.

"Good, Meg," said Jeff.

She tried to relax. Only water gushing against the boat's hull broke the quiet. Breezes tickling her cheek smelled of pine trees.

"Let's tack," said Mr. Anderson. "Ready?"

"I think so." Meg's mouth felt tight and dry.

"Ready," said Jeff.

She brought in more line, and Jeff released one of his lines.

As Mr. Anderson turned the boat, wind swung the sails to the other side. With *Dancer* on a new course, Meg let off her sail a bit. Jeff moved across the boat to tighten his other jib line. *Dancer* tipped farther, slicing the water even faster.

Meg's palms tingled with fear. Jeff and Mr. Anderson sat with her on the high side of the boat. The wind gusted, tilting *Dancer* sharply. Meg cried out and grabbed the lifeline to keep from sliding.

"The mainsail person prevents the boat from capsizing," Mr. Anderson reminded her.

Quickly, Meg let out her line with one hand. The sail slackened, spilling wind. *Dancer* leveled. Meg sighed with relief.

"Try reading the water," said Jeff. "When it darkens with ripples that move toward us, a puff of wind is coming."

Meg eyed an area busy with ripples. Her palms felt clammy as she clutched her line. As the gust hit, she let off her sail, then hauled it in again to maintain speed. She whispered, "I did it!"

Mr. Anderson gave her a thumbs-up sign. "Want to try steering?"

Meg hesitated, then pushed the smooth walnut tiller. *Dancer* pointed into the wind. The sails flapped; the boat slowed. "Oops!" She pulled the tiller toward her, turning the boat until wind filled the sails. Her blood raced as *Dancer* flew.

Back and forth they sailed, crisscrossing the lake. Meg laughed every time water sprayed her. She wanted the afternoon to last forever.

Mr. Anderson tapped her hand. "Will you come again next weekend?"

"Will I!" The thrill of sailing rushed through her like a tidal wave. It washed up memories of running and jumping and everything else the accident had stolen from her. She waited for sadness to clamp around her chest like a boa constrictor. But it didn't. Instead, tears that she hadn't shed since the accident filled her eyes. She covered her face with her hands and sobbed.

After a moment, Mr. Anderson and Jeff hugged her. As *Dancer* headed for the docks, Meg glanced at the glittering water through her tears. She seemed to see a boa constrictor, made of sunlight and shadow, slithering through the ripples.

The sun slipped below the horizon, and the snake sank beneath the lake.

Meg took an easy breath, her deepest in almost a year. Alive, she thought, and free to ride the wind.

"I don't usually cry." She dried her eyes. "I just didn't think I'd ever again be this . . . this . . ." Words caught in her throat.

"This happy?" said Jeff.

She nodded. "This happy."

---

1. Have you ever been discouraged like Meg?

2. Share a time when you helped a friend reach a goal.

3. Is it important to keep doing things that make you feel happy?

Thorgersturm:
Voice in the Storm

By Amy and Robert Cloud

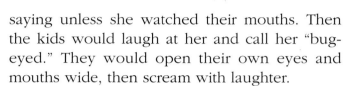

Marie Jonasson looked up with a start from her fourth-grade geography book as a sharp clap of thunder shook the small wooden schoolhouse. For the first time she noticed the air of tension, the fidgeting and murmuring of the students, and the nervous pacing of her teacher, Miss Decker.

"What is it?" Marie whispered to her friend, Anna Bergen.

"It's the *Thorgersturm*—the first big storm of the fall!" Anna replied. "We might have a bad time getting home through this." Marie watched Anna's mouth form the words and nodded agreement.

The principal, Mr. Thurston, came in and spoke briefly to Marie's teacher.

"Children!" Miss Decker said loudly, above the rising whirr of the wind and crash of the surf. "Children, classes are over. The bus-boats are coming early to take you home."

Anna looked at Marie and spoke. "Maybe the storm will keep them from holding school tomorrow, and you can stay at my house." She squeezed her friend's hand, and Marie felt suddenly warm and happy. Anna was one person her own age who wouldn't join the other girls in mocking her.

She had tried to be friendly with the others, but they didn't respond. There was Lauri Ekstrom. "She's from my own island," Marie thought. "I've known her since we were babies, but still Lauri pokes fun at me like everyone else." Marie didn't know why.

They all seemed to speak so softly, even the teachers. She could never tell what they were saying unless she watched their mouths. Then the kids would laugh at her and call her "bug-eyed." They would open their own eyes and mouths wide, then scream with laughter.

But she wasn't trying to be funny with them. She honestly couldn't understand their words most of the time. Sometimes, when they were behind her, she could almost feel their laughter.

The teachers didn't seem to think she was having trouble. In fact, both Miss Inness, who taught first and second grades, and Miss Decker told her parents she did well in class.

"She's a model student," Miss Inness had said. "When she puts down her head to study, nothing disturbs her. She'd go right on reading if the school were falling down."

But the teachers don't know how hard it is for me, Marie thought. When her teacher faced the blackboard or turned aside, she couldn't make out a word the teacher said.

So Marie squeezed Anna's hand, too, and said, "Yes, I hope Dad will let me visit you. I'll ask him when his bus-boat comes in."

The wind howled as the children huddled on the school porch watching for the bus-boats. The principal shouted to the teachers, "I hope the buses get here soon. The phones went out just as Mr. Jonasson said they were starting. This storm gets worse by the minute."

All of a sudden Lauri Ekstrom screamed something, dragging at Mr. Thurston's arm and pointing.

"What's she saying?" Marie asked Anna.

"Look out there at Savo Island. She thinks her dad's motorboat is washed up on the rocks." Marie saw Anna shouting above the storm.

Mr. Thurston rushed inside for a pair of binoculars, with which he quickly scanned the shoreline of tiny Savo.

"It's certainly a capsized boat—and a man is standing by it, waving at us!" Mr. Thurston shouted to the others.

"Let me look!" Lauri tugged at his sleeve until the principal handed her the glasses. "That's Daddy! I knew I recognized our boat. He's trying to say something. See him shouting and waving!"

Mr. Thurston held the binoculars, studying the tiny figure. He finally shook his head and lowered the glasses. "I can't make it out. He's certainly trying to tell us something. But nobody could hear in all this storm."

Marie released Anna's hand. She felt her feet drawing her through the crowd to the principal's side. He had never looked so tall or so stern.

"Please," she said when he bent down, "there is a thing I can do. I—I think I could tell what he's saying."

All eyes were on her as she took the binoculars. With Mr. Thurston's help, she got them focused on Lauri's dad.

She waved an arm frantically. "Go ahead!" she shouted. Perhaps he understood, for he cupped his hands beside his mouth and formed the words, "Can you hear me?"

"Yes! Yes!" She nodded vigorously, waving her free arm at him. Then as he shouted, Marie watched his lips and repeated his words to those around her.

"If any bus-boats arrive—don't board them—stay ashore—Jonasson's boat blew back onto the beach—bus-boats can't float in this storm—I came to warn you—wait there—Coast Guard is coming to rescue."

A big shout went up from the clustered group. Mr. Thurston cupped his hands and shouted back, "We understand."

But no one could hear above the gale's roar, and Mr. Ekstrom continued to shout. Marie said,

"He isn't sure we got it. Let's all go back inside the building, then he'll know we understand."

"Good thinking, Marie!" Mr. Thurston gave her a big grin. "Everybody inside, folks."

At that moment, a heavy coughing chug was added to the storm's roar, as the school's second bus-boat came bucking through the waves. "All aboard. I can't hold her against the dock very long," yelled the pilot.

"Come ashore, Mr. Lewis," the principal called. "The Coast Guard is on the way to rescue us all."

"The boat'll founder!" shouted Mr. Lewis.

"Let her founder!" Mr. Thurston shouted back. "Lives are worth more than boats."

Mr. Lewis jockeyed the bus-boat until it was pointed directly at a small sandy patch, put on full throttle, and drove the bus neatly up onto the shore. He scrambled out with a line and secured the small boat to a tree. Then he ran through the driving rain to shelter.

For the next half-hour the doorway was filled with figures peering anxiously out to sea. Marie found herself beside Lauri, watching Mr. Ekstrom on the tiny island. He had lashed himself to a tree to avoid blowing away.

When the Coast Guard cutter appeared from the midst of the storm and took Nels Ekstrom aboard, the whole school cheered.

Lauri hugged Marie and turned up her face so her words could be seen.

"Marie, you were wonderful. You saved us all."

Marie glowed as she returned Lauri's hug.

---

1. Do you ever imagine that someday you might be a hero?

2. Do you think that a small deed of bravery is as important as a big one?

3. Have you ever been challenged and wanted to quit? Did you quit, or did you keep trying?

Cartwheels

I can't turn cartwheels. I've tried and tried.
I can start. I can get about halfway . . .
Then I buckle over somehow and collapse
sideways.

I told Mother. "Practice," she advised.
I said I had. It didn't work. I just plain couldn't
do them.

"Well, you can write poems," she said,
"And you're so good at math . . ."
She went on and on and it was all very nice.
I appreciated it.

I still can't turn cartwheels.

Jean Little

Tryouts

If I try out,
what's the worst?
The worst is
I might lose,
not be the one they choose.

I could say it didn't matter;
I was kidding when I tried.
Then everyone would know
I lost and then I lied.

Or I could shrug and say,
"So what, I lost,
I'm only a beginner."
Besides,
if I never try,
I'll never be a winner.

Sara Holbrook

The Way Things Are

It's today,
    This road,
    This knowing the road is there.
    A few brambles,
    A few tangles,
    A few scratches,
    A rough stone against your toe,
    But still, you've got to go
    And take it.
    Fast, sometimes,
    Or slow,
    But go—
    everywhere.
    anywhere
    You need
    to go.

Myra Cohn Livingston

Time to Play

Mama says to play outside.
Wish I had a bike to ride.
I'll fly to the moon instead.
Steer the rocket in my head.
I'll pretend to find a star
no one else has seen so far.
Then I'll name it after me—
    Africa Lawanda Lee!
But for now I'll grab some chalk,
play hopscotch out on the walk.

Nikki Grimes

I Did It!

Young patients at a pediatric rehabilitation hospital ask occasionally if they may stay until they come of age. For them, the hospital staff and fellow patients become a family of sorts.

So, too, are the pensioners at the Paris inn owned by Mirette's widowed mother in *Mirette on the High Wire* (McCully). In befriending an aerialist who has lost his nerve and supporting him at a critical moment, Mirette discovers her own courage—to take a risk by walking on the high wire above the streets of Paris.

Mirette's story was given to a young patient who did not want to leave the hospital. *Identifying with the main character helped to bolster the girl's belief in her abilities* to manage her own medical care. "Mirette was scared on the high wire," said the patient. "But she did it anyway."

Two Hundred and Fifty Steps

By Harriett Diller
and Betty Hodges

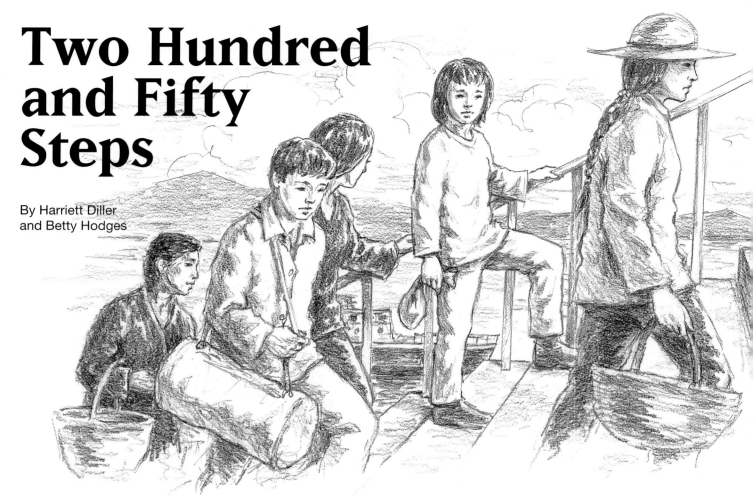

The January cold sliced through Gao Ling's windbreaker as she stood on the deck of the *East Wind 37*. Few passengers on the steamboat were willing to put up with the biting wind that whipped off the river today. Gao Ling was glad. Being alone here at the bow was like riding down the Yangtze in her own private boat.

The door behind her creaked open, and Mother stepped out onto the deck. "We should make it to Wuhan in good time," she said, smiling. Mother always worried that they would get fogged in during the three-day trip down the river and be late for the New Year's celebration at Grandfather's house. "Come in out of the cold now."

"But I love to watch the river," Gao Ling said. She never tired of the scenery along the Yangtze. This part of the river had high cliffs on one side and flat rocks on the other. Lonely evergreens perched on the hills.

She didn't want to be inside the *East Wind* where children cried and roosters crowed.

The thick smell of food cooking hung in the air all day long. Inside, Gao Ling would have to face the people. The other passengers were full of questions. Where was her home? Where was she going? Gao Ling could never find the courage to answer.

"Can't I stay outside a little bit longer?" she asked Mother.

"No," Mother said. "I have an errand for you to run in Wanxian. We'll be docking any minute."

An errand. Mother had never sent her on an errand in Wanxian. "Alone?"

"Gao Ling, you're old enough now to go into Wanxian and buy oranges for Grandfather."

"From a street vendor?"

"Of course from a street vendor. Who else?" Mother sighed. "Gao Ling, you've got to stop being so shy. You hang your head. You won't look at people. You're even scared to run errands. A big girl like you."

"Can't you at least go with me into Wanxian?" Gao Ling asked.

Mother shook her head and dug a few coins out of her pocket. "I don't feel up to climbing those steps today."

When the *East Wind 37* docked at Wanxian, passengers crowded off the boat to begin the long climb into town. Two hundred and fifty steps stretched up the cliff. Today Gao Ling didn't mind the slippery steps. She would have climbed these steps forever if it meant she didn't have to buy the oranges.

Too soon, Gao Ling reached the top. The main street of Wanxian was just as muddy as the steps. Everywhere men sat peeling oranges and tossing the peels into boxes. People laughed. Vendors stuffed squawking chickens into net bags. Voices shouted out for customers. "This must be the noisiest place in China," Gao Ling thought. If only she could be on her own private steamboat sailing down the silent Yangtze. Away from the noise. Away from the people.

One vendor's shrill voice rose above the others. It belonged to the woman selling oranges on the other side of the marketplace. Gao Ling remembered her from other years— her crooked brown teeth, the black of her eyes melting into the white. Before, Gao Ling had always crouched behind Mother so that she wouldn't have to talk to the vendor.

"Buy my lucky oranges?" the woman asked as Gao Ling walked toward her.

"Speak," Gao Ling urged herself. "Speak!" But she couldn't say the words. Instead, she turned and skated across the mud, away from the vendor, away from Wanxian, down to the *East Wind 37*.

Back aboard the boat, Gao Ling found her mother lying on her cot. "Where are Grandfather's oranges?" asked Mother.

"I didn't get them," Gao Ling whispered.

"You know Grandfather looks forward to Wanxian oranges all year."

Gao Ling was ashamed of herself. A *big girl like you*, her mother had said. Too scared to buy oranges from a street vendor.

That night fog covered the river, and the next morning it still hung like a ghost around the *East Wind 37*.

"We're fogged in," Mother said. "We'll never make it to Wuhan by New Year's now." She sighed and lay back down on her cot.

Everything was going wrong. The ship was fogged in. Mother didn't feel well enough to climb the steps into Wanxian. Grandfather wouldn't have any oranges for New Year's. "I should do something," Gao Ling thought.

Gao Ling knew what she must do. She must climb the two hundred and fifty steps into Wanxian. She knew the *East Wind 37* wouldn't leave without her. She had heard the captain say it couldn't sail until the fog lifted.

Gao Ling went ashore and climbed through the fog, up into Wanxian. Fog masked the marketplace so that she couldn't see anything. The crowd of shoppers, the chicken vendors, the boxes of orange peels—it was as if they weren't there.

Then Gao Ling heard her. A shrill voice pierced through the fog like the cry of a chicken. "Oranges. Buy my lucky oranges." Gao Ling made herself walk toward the voice.

"I can do it," Gao Ling thought, fingering the coins in her pocket. "Ten oranges, please," she said, hoping the vendor didn't notice the quiver in her voice.

Gao Ling paid the woman and stuffed the oranges carefully into her net bag. As she slid away down the muddy street, the sun peeked through the fog. The *East Wind 37* would sail today after all. They would be only a little late getting to Grandfather's house. She was sure of that.

"Wait till Mother sees what's in my bag," Gao Ling said to herself. Hurrying down the steps toward the Yangtze, she felt as light as the east wind.

---

1. Have you felt shy in certain situations?

2. Has it helped to think about other people rather than yourself?

3. Can you be scared and brave at the same time? If so, how can this be?

Fergus Has Spoken!

By Harriett Diller

Fergus Mackey had plenty to say. But Fergus spoke so softly that no one ever heard him.

At supper one night Fergus said, "Please pass the peas."

"Who do you think will win the basketball championship?" Father asked Fergus's big brother, Angus.

"I hear it's supposed to rain tomorrow," Mother said.

"Can we go to the park after supper?" the triplets, Robert, Hugh, and Matthew, yelled.

"I think I'll finish off these peas," said Fergus's big sister, Margaret.

At school the next day Fergus's teacher, Mrs. Corona, asked a question. "Can anyone name the planets of our Solar System?"

"Mercury, Venus, Earth, Mars, Jupiter, Saturn, Uranus, Neptune, and Pluto," said Fergus.

"Surely someone must know," said Mrs. Corona. "Well, class, I'd say you need to study your science books more carefully."

"I do study my science book," Fergus said. "Science is my best subject."

But of course no one heard him.

Fergus was fed up. When school was over he stalked straight home to his laboratory in the garage. He found an old portable radio, some wire, six *D* batteries, and a few other parts he'd found at the junkyard.

"I'll show everybody," he said. "I'll invent a Super Deluxe Voice Amplifier and Screen Machine. Then people will listen to me."

The family cat, Walter, rubbed against his leg. Fergus knew that was Walter's way of asking, "How does it work?"

"See, Walter, it knows the sound waves of my voice. It screens out all other sound waves

64

so my voice gets heard above the others."

Fergus worked until it was time for bed. Then he hung his great invention over his shoulder with an old suitcase strap and started into the house.

At breakfast the next morning Fergus said, "Please pass the eggs."

"I hear it's supposed to be hot and humid today," said Mother.

Fergus turned up the volume of his Super Deluxe Voice Amplifier and Screen Machine. He cleared his throat. "Please pass the eggs."

Everyone stared at him.

"Fergus has spoken!" Father cried. "Somebody pass him the eggs."

"Will this be enough?" brother Angus said, passing the bowl.

"I could run to the store and get some more," Margaret offered.

"I'd be happy to borrow some eggs from the neighbors," Mother said.

"Here. Take some of mine," said one of the triplets.

"No, mine," said the other two triplets.

"That's all right," Fergus told them. "I have plenty now."

Fergus was thrilled with the way his invention was working. He turned it off to save the batteries. "I can't wait to try it out at school this morning."

At school Mrs. Corona asked, "Has anyone memorized Lincoln's Gettysburg Address yet?"

Fergus had memorized it days earlier, and no one had been able to hear him. But that was before his Super Deluxe Voice Amplifier and Screen Machine.

"Four score and seven years ago . . .," Fergus began, and recited the Gettysburg Address from beginning to end.

Mrs. Corona's mouth flew open. "Fergus has spoken!"

"Bravo!" the class cried.

"Encore! More!"

So Fergus also recited the Preamble to the Constitution and a poem called "Daffodils."

The whole class applauded.

"Magnificent!"

"Astounding!"

Finally Fergus was done. He gave his Super Deluxe Amplifier and Screen Machine a pat. "Couldn't have done it without you," he whispered. He reached to turn it off to save the batteries.

That's when Fergus noticed. He'd forgotten to turn on his invention when he arrived at school.

"You mean I recited the Gettysburg Address and the Preamble to the Constitution and 'Daffodils' all by myself and everybody heard me?"

That gave Fergus something to think about.

Ever since that day, when Fergus Mackey speaks, people listen.

---

1. Have you ever worried that you might not be able to change a habit?

2. Has it helped to approach a solution from a different angle?

3. When you have solved a personal problem, are you surprised that family and friends are happy for you?

I Did It!

I did it!
I did it!
Come and look
At what I've done!
I read a book!
When someone wrote it
Long ago
For me to read,
How did he know
That this was the book
I'd take from the shelf
And lie on the floor
And read by myself?
I really read it!
Just like that!
Word by word,
From first to last!
I'm sleeping with
This book in bed,
This first FIRST book
I've ever read!

David Harrison

Girls Can, Too!

Tony said: "Boys are better!
They can . . .

 whack a ball,
 ride a bike with one hand
 leap off a wall."

I just listened
 and when he was through,
I laughed and said:

 "Oh, yeah! Well, girls can, too!"

Then I leaped off the wall,
 and rode away
With *his* 200 baseball cards
 I won that day.

Lee Bennett Hopkins

The Test

It's not my fault if I flunked the test.
This room's too cold to do my best.
My foot's asleep,
I lost my gum,
I've got a fever,
This pencil's dumb,
My collar's tight,
There's a pain in my head,
I couldn't hear
A thing you said,
My throat is sore,
I need a drink,
Billy's humming,
I can't think,
And . . .
What's that! You say I passed the test?
Well, if I do say so, I did my best.

David Harrison

Hey World, Here I Am!

I said to the World, "I've arrived.
I, Kate Bloomfield, have come at last."
The World paid no attention.
I said to the World, "Hey World, here I am!
Don't you understand?
It's me, Kate Bloomfield."
The World ignored me.
I took myself off into a corner.
"Guess what?" I whispered. "I made it.
You know . . . Kate Bloomfield."
My Self bellowed, "YeaaaAAY, Kate!"
And spun six somersaults up the middle of Main
Street.
The World turned.
"What did you say?" said the World.
I paid no attention.
After all, I gave it its chance.
It's not my fault that it missed me.

Jean Little

That's What Friends are For

An older brother felt responsible for his younger brother's serious bicycling accident and refused to talk about it. In *On My Honor* (Bauer) he identified with the character, Joel, and Joel's guilt feelings over his best friend's accidental drowning during a bike outing. Through the story this older brother was *given a channel for releasing his own emotions* and for diminishing his sense of isolation—someone else had had a like experience and felt the same sense of loss, guilt, and responsibility.

The mother of the two boys told hospital staff that her older son had not only read *On My Honor*, but had felt motivated to give a book report on it in school.

Nice Guys Win, Too

By Joann Mazzio

"**W**esley's my best friend. I don't want to wrestle him," I said to Kathy. We were waiting for the school bus.

I had known Kathy forever. I didn't know anyone else who was as good at listening to my problems.

"What if I hurt him?" I asked.

"You won't," Kathy said. "When you two wrestle for fun, you're about even. Sometimes you win, sometimes Wes does."

Today's match wasn't just for fun, though. Today was for the school championship.

"Wesley *needs* to win," I said. "That's the real problem."

Kathy looked puzzled.

"I've been to dinner at his house lots of times," I said. "At the table, his father seems to keep scores in his head. He starts with the oldest kid and asks them all what they did that day. He means in sports. He jumps right over Wesley because Wes doesn't have anything to say."

Kathy interrupted, "What about the young ones? Are they in sports, too?"

"Sure," I said. "All of them. The family's trophy case is bigger than the one at school."

"I fear you exaggerate, young man," Kathy said, imitating our teacher. "You're not thinking about giving up, are you?"

I shook my head. "Wes wouldn't want to win that way. But I'll feel bad if I win."

"Haven't you heard?" Kathy said. "Nice guys finish last."

I thought about the wrestling match all morning. When we went outside after lunch, I was still worried and not paying attention. Jake caught me off guard with a snowball to my chest.

Wes laughed and scooped up a snowball. He let it fly at Jake, but it hit the principal, Mr. Powers, who had just stepped out of the cafeteria. I was still patting a lump of snow in my hands.

In his office, Mr. Powers opened his big

70

notebook where he keeps track of bad behavior.

"Jacob," he said, "this is the third time I've had you in here for throwing snowballs. I'll have to call your parents for a conference. Wait outside, please."

Mr. Powers flipped more pages. "Wes and Ben, this is your second visit here. The first time was a problem with bubble gum, I see." He wasn't smiling.

Wes and I sat stiffly on the wooden chairs. We didn't smile either.

I heard a sniffle from Wes. A tear ran down his cheek.

I was surprised. We'd been caught doing something wrong and there would have to be punishment. But we were sixth graders. Sixth graders don't cry over something like this.

Mr. Powers didn't call our parents. He warned us, though. One more mark in his book and we'd be in real trouble.

After school all the kids gathered in the gym to watch the wrestling finals. When it was our turn, Wes and I shook hands, then went at each other with all our strength. After two periods, we were tied with seven points each.

One more period. Just two more minutes to go. I was still worried. I wanted to win. But I wanted Wes to win, too. Wes should have something to tell his dad at dinner.

The kids yelled encouragement.

"Come on, Ben, you can do it," Kathy said.

"Hang in there, Wes," called Jeff.

Wes grinned at me, but he looked determined. He dropped to his hands and knees in the middle of the mat in the starting position.

I wiped my sweaty hands on my jersey. I knelt on one knee and put my open hand on Wes's elbow. My other hand went around his waist.

We waited for the whistle. It seemed like a long time.

Wes's body was rigid.

A drop of sweat trickled down my cheek. It reminded me of . . . tears. Suddenly something flashed into my mind—something that would make me the winner.

Wes's ear was inches from my mouth. All I had to do was whisper one word in Wes's ear: crybaby! If I could get him off guard for just one second, I could pin him.

One word, and I could win.

The whistle blew. Wes tried to sit back against me. I pushed into him and tried to knock him off balance. I almost got him down, but he pushed hard with his legs and escaped. One point for Wes.

I threw myself at his legs and brought him down again. Two points for me. But he quickly broke my hold and got another point. We were tied again.

We were both sweating, both trying as hard as we could. Time flew by. Wes didn't give me any more openings. Finally he brought me down. I was fast enough to roll onto my stomach, but he still had control. And he had two more points.

I couldn't escape. Why hadn't I said the word? I'd have been the winner by now.

The whistle blew. Coach held up Wes's hand. "Good match, guys," he said.

We walked off the mat. Kathy patted me on the back. "Nice going, Ben. You wrestled real good, Mr. Nice Guy." She was smiling, not sarcastic.

I smiled back, unsnapping my headgear. "Nice guys can be winners, too," I said.

---

1. Is it true that "sticks and stones may break my bones, but names will never hurt me"?

2. Have you ever known something about a friend that could hurt your friend if you used it against her or him? What prevented you from doing so?

3. Are there other situations where someone might try hard not to make a remark to hurt a friend?

The Homecoming

By Maria Testa

I stared at myself in the bathroom mirror. "Practice!" I said out loud. "You need practice!" I held my face steady and studied my reflection. Eyes straight ahead, jaw square, mouth even—good! I turned around and stood with my back to the mirror. Now for a tough one:

Mary-Margaret comes home, you go to meet her in front of her house, and . . . she looks like a monster from a horror show.

I whirled around to look at my reflection. No expression. Good. Okay now, one more time:

Mary-Margaret comes home, you look at her for the first time, and . . . she looks like a space alien from a science-fiction movie.

I whipped around again to check my reflection. Same blank expression. Great. Maybe I was ready.

Suddenly I realized that there was another face in the mirror.

It was Dad, standing in the doorway, carrying an armload of fresh towels. Poor Dad. He looked as if he thought his only daughter had lost her mind. I had to tell him something. I chose the truth.

"Hi, Dad," I said. "I'm just practicing for when Mary-Margaret comes home from the hospital tomorrow." He looked at me kind of funny. I have to admit I sounded pretty dumb.

"Vanessa," he said, "Mary-Margaret has lived next door to us for ten years. Have you always practiced before going over to visit her?"

"Come on, Dad!" I heard my voice rising. "You know this is different. I don't even know what she's going to look like. Mrs. Redding said the firecracker went off right in Mary-Margaret's face! What if her whole face was burned off?"

I was shaking. Up until then, I don't think I knew how scared I was.

"I'm sorry, hon," Dad whispered as I buried my face in the towels he was carrying. "But just remember, no matter what she looks like, she's still Mary-Margaret."

"I know," I said, lifting my head so he could hear me. "That's what I keep telling myself. I just want to be ready if, you know, she really looks awful."

"You will be, Vanessa," Dad said softly. "You're the best best friend in the world."

I wished I were so sure.

The next morning I watched my reflection carefully as I brushed my teeth in front of the bathroom mirror. No more practicing, I said to myself. No more games. You're just going next door to see Mary-Margaret. No big deal.

I was outside waiting when the Reddings' car pulled up in front of their house. I could tell Mary-Margaret was sitting in the back seat, but I couldn't quite see her face.

"Vanessa!" Mrs. Redding called to me as she stepped out of the car. "How nice of you to greet us."

I waited for Mary-Margaret to get out next. But she didn't. Why was she staying in the car?

I looked at Mrs. Redding, searching for some kind of clue. But she just smiled at me and nodded slightly. Then she went inside.

That's when it hit me. I was so worried about how I would react to Mary-Margaret that I hadn't given any thought to how she would feel about being seen. I knew it was up to me to make the first move.

I walked up to the half-open car window. Mary-Margaret sat very still in the back seat, her face turned away from me.

"Hi, Mary-Margaret," I said.

"Go away," she said quietly. "I don't want you to see my face."

I felt my throat tighten, but I made myself talk. "I just wanted to say that I'm happy you're home."

Mary-Margaret was silent for a moment. Then she turned toward me slowly.

"I'm going to be okay, you know," she said. "The doctors say it will take a long time, but I am going to get better."

"I'm so glad," I whispered. I didn't mean to, but I couldn't stop staring. She didn't look at all like any kind of monster or space alien. Her face was almost completely covered with loose bandages, and most of her hair was gone.

It was then that I figured out who she looked like. She looked like Mary-Margaret, my best friend, after a terrible accident.

I wanted to tell her that everything was going to be fine. I wanted to tell her how much I had missed her. But I couldn't. Instead, I did something really stupid and awful and absolutely wonderful.

I laughed.

And I didn't just giggle or anything. I mean, I really cracked up. I don't know why, exactly. Maybe it was because I was scared, or maybe it was because I was just so happy that my best friend was finally home.

"Stop laughing at me!" Mary-Margaret said, but she didn't really sound angry.

"I'm sorry!" I blurted out as I gasped for air. "I'm not laughing at you . . . I don't know why I'm laughing. I'm just so happy you're home!"

Then Mary-Margaret started to laugh, too. We both laughed so hard that the next thing I knew tears were streaming down my cheeks, and we didn't know if we were laughing or crying.

"It's okay," Mary-Margaret said. I could see her smile behind the bandages. "You know," she said, "I didn't think I'd ever say this, but I really missed your stupid laugh!"

Mary-Margaret climbed out of the car and put an arm around my shoulders. We marched through the Reddings' front door, together, still laughing. I knew for sure we were the best best friends in the world.

---

1. Have you ever known someone who has had a change in appearance?

2. Did you want to stay away from that person?

3. What would help you to remain friends?

The New Neighbor

I see your hair is in a braid.
I like to wear mine that way, too.
You say you've finished second
grade.
Well, funny, I've just finished, too.

You say your sisters are a pain.
My brothers make my day a mess.
You say you like to walk in rain.
Well, I like rain some, too, I guess.

Why don't you come and visit me?
I've lots of toys and books to lend.
I think it's really plain to see
that you were meant to be my
friend.

Marci Ridlon

From Some Things Go Together

Hats with heads
Pillows with beds

Franks with beans
Kings with queens

Lions with zoo
and me with you

White with snow
Wind with blow

Moon with night
Sun with light

Sky with blue
AND ME WITH YOU!

Charlotte Zolotow

The most
I can do for
my friend is
simply to be
his friend.

Henry David Thoreau

If you don't come

The sun will get
smaller and smaller
and the grass won't green
or the trees leaf
and there will be
no flowers or birdsong.

The winds will blow cold
and the nights will be dark
without moonlight or stars

for there will be
no summer here
if you don't come.

Marguerite Mack

Finding Peace—or Making It!

Armed intruders entered an elementary school near Chicago. Their gun shots wounded two students and a teacher, ending the sense of security and peaceful learning that the school had offered to its students and staff.

In the ensuing days, an English teacher looked in the school library for a book that she could read to her classes—a book that would offer calmness and reassurance. *Sarah, Plain and Tall* (MacLachlan) was her excellent choice. Learning to love again, completing a broken family circle, and cherishing song in the setting of the quiet, flowering prairie offered a sense of tranquility to the children in her classes. *Sometimes it is best not to mirror a problem, but to suggest a healing process.*

No Man's Land

By Susan Campbell Bartoletti

Micah Jenkins cracked open the leather-bound diary his ma had given him before he marched out of Oglethorpe last spring. *November 30, 1862*, he wrote. *We still await orders. Our regiment had one extra drill for making sport of the drummer. Went on picket duty.*

Micah sighed as he slipped the diary into his haversack. More than once older soldiers had told him that a fourteen-year-old boy should be home, waiting for whiskers to sprout. Instead, here he stood near the Rappahannock River, guarding against the tinkling of cowbells and other calls that could turn into Yankee scouts.

"Hello, Reb!" came a call across the stream.

"Hello, Yank," answered Jules, another Rebel picket.

"We're getting water."

"Go ahead. We won't look."

Micah recognized the voice. It belonged to the Yankee whom he had met earlier as they both gathered firewood from the same rail fence. The boy couldn't have been any older than Micah. "Now we'll be drinking from opposite sides of the same stream," he thought.

After a few splashes, the Yankee called again, "Hey, Reb."

"Yeah, Yank?"

"We left a little something for your trouble."

The brush crackled as the Union soldiers left. Micah ran to the water's edge and plucked a small, crudely built boat from the reeds. He took out coffee and nuts. The other pickets whooped with joy and took turns sniffing the coffee beans.

"Seems strange to have Yanks camped so close," said Micah.

"After Malvern Hill my regiment fell upon some Yankees picking blueberries," said Jules.

"What happened?" asked Micha.

Jules chuckled. "We called our own truce and spent the morning picking berries together." He paused, then added, "Of course, we picked more than they did."

"We've sneaked across picket lines to play

cards with Yanks," said Charley. "Beat them every time."

"That's nothing," said Goodloe. "Once we held a swimming party with a company of Bluecoats. There's nothing uglier than a white-bellied Yankee—unless it's a blue-bellied one."

As the pickets laughed, Micah wondered, "If it weren't for the war, might we be friends with those Yanks?" He wished he had something to give them, but all his haversack held was his diary, a mess kit, a jackknife, a mending kit, and a ball of darning yarn.

Suddenly he had an idea. He took a Minie ball from the ammunition box and wound his darning yarn tightly around it until it was as big as his fist. Then he knotted it. On a piece of paper he scrawled "good sport" and pinned it to the ball.

He ran down to the water. "Hey Yank," he called. "Here's something for you."

The bushes rustled, and then the young Yankee appeared on the bank. Micah tossed the ball across. The Yankee caught it and smiled as he read the note.

"We've got a hickory rail for a bat," said the Yankee. "How many good sports are there in that sorry-looking camp of yours?"

"Enough to give you the best whupping you ever got," Goodloe hollered.

The Yankees laughed, and a harmonica sang out "Yankee Doodle." Charley's harmonica retaliated with a chorus of "Dixie."

The next day the Rebels and the Yankees faced each other in "No Man's Land," the clearing that lay between the lines. Behind each team the flags were hoisted high. Between them, the white flag of truce fluttered.

Gripping the yarn ball, Micah eyed the Yankee's hickory-rail bat and tossed the ball. The Yankee smacked the ball. A Rebel scooped up the ball and aimed for the Yankee. Too late. The Yank was safe at first.

By the third inning, the Yankees led, 23-22, with Jules on second base. Both sides groaned as they saw that the yarn ball had unraveled to a pile of thread.

"Find a rock," suggested Goodloe.

The Yankees and Rebels scoured the field.

"Here, Reb," a Yankee yelled, tossing a walnut-sized rock in the air. A Rebel wadded the yarn around the rock. Another Yankee peeled off his sock and dropped the yarn-and-rock wadding into it. Cheering, the teams quickly fell into their places.

The hickory rail felt splintery in Micah's hands as he stood, feet planted and eyes locked on the pitcher. The Yankee tossed the sock-ball. Micah swung. *Whack!* His heart pounding, he dug for first base, then on to second. Jules rounded third base, then sped for home. Dirt flying, he hit home, tying the score at 23. Shouts and cheers rang out.

Micah tensed, ready to run as the next batter faced the pitcher, but just as the pitcher brought his arm back, the Rebel bugle sounded, calling the men to formation. As the white flag was lowered, Micah's eyes met the Yankee's who had caught the yarn ball across the stream. The two boys raised their hands in salute, then quietly followed the men from "No-Man's-Land."

That night more fires lit the fields like fallen stars. Micah listened as the Yankees across the stream sang "Home Sweet Home." One by one, the Rebel pickets joined in.

Micah took out his diary and wrote, *December 1, 1862. Reinforcements have arrived. We're ordered to keep in readiness all night.*

---

1. Have you been surprised to find that you can like someone whom you considered an enemy? Or a rival group such as kids from another school, another team, or another neighborhood?

2. What does this story tell you about soldiers in a war?

3. How do you think Micah will feel when the fighting starts again?

Neighbors from Cucumbers

By Marcella Fisher Anderson

Mom and I had just finished our supper one evening when a pickup truck came clanging down our road. From the kitchen window we watched a family unloading their truck in the driveway and moving into the house that had been vacant for three years.

"Who are they?" I asked.

"Migrant workers, I hear," said Mom.

"Migrant workers?" I asked. "What's that?"

"Folks who move around from crop to crop and hire out to pick the harvest. Mostly they live in camps, but these folks seem to have scraped up enough money to buy the old house." Mom's thin lips tightened. "I wish them luck moving into this town. People aren't very friendly, especially to newcomers."

After I finished washing the dishes, I walked out the back door. A boy my age stood by the truck.

"Hello," I said. "Where you from?"

"Cucumbers," he replied, scarcely looking up. "And before that, peas. But we're not movin' on to potatoes this year. Papa says not. He's got himself a steady job in the sawmill."

"My name's Will," I said. "What's yours?"

"Juan."

"What grade are you in?"

"First," he said.

"First! Why, you're as big as I am."

"I know, but I never had a chance to go to real school before."

That did it. I wasn't going to pal around with a boy my size, only in first grade. "See you later," I said.

Usually, Mom made a loaf of her good bread for new neighbors, but I noticed she didn't start that night, or any night. I didn't see anyone visit them, either.

So I stayed away from the house and spent the time on my bike, puttering around the back roads and fishing when I could. The biggest trout I ever saw kept escaping me that summer. But the truth was, I was lonesome. I felt cheated, too, that the first boy my age to move near was so different. With Mom working and us living outside of town, the days were long. Though I pretended the house next door wasn't there, I couldn't help but notice the family working hard in their garden.

It was the best garden I ever saw. They made neat rows by tying string between opposite stakes when they seeded. And when the peas ripened, they stripped those vines so fast I couldn't see their hands move.

One night I was in bed, nearly asleep, when I heard strange sounds in the yard next door. I climbed out of bed. Carefully, I tried to raise the window shade, but of course it snapped up. By the time I looked out, everything was still. So I gave up and went back to bed. I must have slept, because the next thing I heard was feet running hard over the dirt driveway away from the house.

The next morning the sun came in early on account of my snapped-up window shade, and I saw everything real clear. First off, I noticed the corn had been broken in half and carrots pulled up and thrown about and squash vines torn into pieces. It wasn't woodchucks but another kind of animal that did this. A pair of grown-up shoeprints in the dirt proved it.

Mom sat me down for a breakfast I couldn't eat. Halfway through my juice I heard the pickup truck next door start up and drive away. "They didn't want to go on," I said, "to potatoes or beets or anything."

"What kind of talk is that?" Mom asked. "Is that the only way those folks can talk about moving from place to place?" Then she started to cry.

"Who did it?" I demanded.

Mom shook her head.

"Maybe we all did it," I said loudly. "Not one of us was friendly to them. We should at least have tried. We were their closest neighbors."

Mom wiped her eyes on a dish towel.

I left my egg half-eaten and walked outside. I didn't know what to do, so I just stared at the garden. Pretty soon I went to the shed and got out a rake.

Mom called the police. An officer came out and wrote things down. Word got around pretty fast after that.

Folks we hadn't seen for a long time came over and just raked alongside me. Some brought seedlings from their own gardens. Where there was a chance for a second crop, we reseeded. Nobody laughed or told jokes.

After a while the garden began to look pretty good again. I stood up to stretch and saw the sun warm and mellow in the sky.

We heard the muffler on the pickup truck before we saw it coming down the road and turning into the driveway. Juan's father climbed out of the cab, but he kept his hand on the door handle. He looked at the garden and at all of us. Then he stared at his feet. He didn't say anything—just opened the truck door—and the rest of the family climbed out and walked slowly into the house. He looked at me then, and I thought I saw a flicker of a smile on his face.

Everyone else started drifting away. It seemed suddenly chilly with them going. A slight breeze moved the new plants in the garden.

Suddenly, I didn't think I could stand it anymore—not joining up with a kid my own age right next door. I didn't say anything to Mom. I just walked over to the house. When I knocked on the door, Juan came right out, so he must have watched me coming.

"I have this bike," I said, as though he'd never seen me ride it. "Do you have a bike?"

His lips parted in a small smile. "I have one—not very good. I brought it from cucumbers."

"You don't mean from cucumbers," I said. "You mean from the place where you picked cucumbers. You've got to learn to talk like the rest of us if you're ever going to catch up in school."

He nodded, and a bright light came into his eyes.

"Let's go riding right after supper," I said. I thought his smile would never stop. "And tomorrow," I went on, "I'll take you to a pond where there's the biggest trout you ever saw."

---

1. Do you find it hard to be a friend with someone from a background that is different from your own?

2. What could you do to help break down such a barrier?

3. What are some of the difficulties when you try to make friends with someone who speaks differently from you, eats food you find strange, and has customs that are unfamiliar to you?

Night

Stars over snow,
  And in the west a planet
Swinging below a star—
  Look for a lovely thing and you will find it,
It is not far—
  It never will be far.

Sara Teasdale

Angry

Sometimes when the day is bad
And someone's made me very mad
Or I've been given angry stares,
I go behind the front porch stairs.

There, curled up with chin on knee,
I like to be alone with me
And listen to the people talk
And hurry by me on the walk.

There I sit, without a sound,
And draw stick pictures on the ground.
If I should tire of it all,
I throw some pebbles at the wall.

After I've been there awhile
And find that I can almost smile,
I brush me off and count to ten
And try to start the day again.

Marci Ridlon

Orders

Muffle the wind;
Silence the clock;
Muzzle the mice;
Curb the small talk;
Cure the hinge-squeak;
Banish the thunder.
Let me sit silent,
Let me wonder.

A.M. Klein

City Snow

How still it is. How soundless!
No noises from the streets.
No dumpsters clang. Police cars drive
along snow-muffled beats.

A frosty arctic light
leaks out onto my sill,
seeks hiding places of the night.
The creaking eaves are still.

I raise the shade. Snow fills
the sky! A shering pigeon drops
and slides on ice. No footprints
lead to parks or coffee shops.

This means, I guess, there'll be
no school, no basketball to play.
I'll pull my covers up and
be as quiet as the day.

Marcella Fisher Anderson

Tomorrow Will Be Better

A grandson in first grade was being tutored in reading to help him overcome a learning disability. In the hope of encouraging him and knowing he loved animals, his grandmother read him the picture book edition of *Lassie Come Home* (Wells). He heard the classic dog story where love, daring, persistence, and struggle helped Lassie to reach home again. *Stories that conclude successfully can help to encourage a child who is struggling with learning a new skill.*

WHAT WILL HAPPEN TO DOBBIE?

By Elizabeth Van Steenwyk

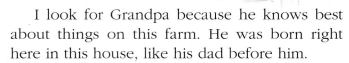

When I go to Grandma and Grandpa's farm, I like to ride Dobbie best. But I won't be going there after today. After today the farm won't be theirs anymore.

Today, Grandma and Grandpa are having a sale. They are selling the farm and everything on it. Not because they want to. They have to. Then they will move into town and live with us.

Times are bad, Mom says. Times are real bad for farmers. Farmers are losing everything, Dad says. Bales of hay from the barn, chairs from the house, even Grandma's tub of prize petunias will be sold before the day is over.

The sale has already begun. Out here in the barnyard a man is standing on a big box in front of a lot of people. Some of them are neighbors. Some of them are friends. A few of them are strangers. They've all come to buy something or maybe just to watch. Maybe some of them will have a sale one day soon, too. That man on the box is talking so fast I can't understand him. But I guess other people do, because someone just bought Grandpa's lawn mower.

"Sold," says the man on the box. So I guess it's true.

Then I have a terrible thought that makes the day turn gray. Not pretty pearly gray, but ugly, urpy gray.

Is that man up there going to sell Dobbie, too? He can't sell old Dobbie to strangers. Dobbie's been our pony all his life. I ride him everytime I visit. I've got to ask. What will happen to Dobbie?

I look for Grandpa because he knows best about things on this farm. He was born right here in this house, like his dad before him.

I see him standing over by his tractor, patting it kind of soft and gentle with his old, sandpapery hands. I decide not to ask him just now. He needs to pat his tractor some more, all by himself.

I find Daddy next, talking to some men.

"Dad." I pull on his jacket sleeve. "I have something to ask. It's real important."

"Not now, Catherine," he says. "Right now I have to give everyone these lists of things to be sold." He hands out pieces of paper to people standing around.

I wonder if Dobbie is on that list.

Then I decide that Grandma will know about Dobbie, so I go inside where some ladies are talking. I can hear them way outside.

Grandma's circle ladies from church are serving food in the dining room. Doughnuts, homemade rolls, cake and pie, good stuff like that.

"Have a doughnut, Catherine," someone says.

I love doughnuts, but not now. Not until I know about Dobbie.

There's Grandma, giving away home-canned jars of green beans. Grandma always has a basement full of home-canned stuff from her garden. But not anymore because she's giving it all away.

It won't make me mad to see the beans go, but I hope she'll keep some jars of peaches and strawberry jam to eat at our house.

So I go looking for Mom and find her in the living room, helping with the sale of quilts that Grandma made over the years. She made one for me for Christmas this year. It has sixteen bears on it, and I get to keep it. But the rest of the quilts have to be sold, because Grandma and Grandpa need the money. Grandma says not to be sad, she can always make more quilts, now that she'll have plenty of time.

Everyone's too busy to talk about Dobbie, so I go out to the barn to talk to him instead.

There he is, standing against the stall gate, waiting for his afternoon carrot.

"Sorry, Dobbie." I scratch behind his ears where he likes it best. "Today's different. No carrot."

Some men come into the barn. One by one they lead Tessa and Florence and Abigail from their stalls. It looks as if someone is going to buy Gran's best milk cows, too.

Suddenly I have an idea. Maybe if I stay with Dobbie, people with think I've bought him and they'll leave him here. Maybe they'll even forget about him until the sale is over. It's worth a try.

I climb over the gate and into Dobbie's stall. Then I begin to brush his old brown coat and his dirty white mane. His face has lots of gray hair on it now. I wonder if his skin underneath is as wrinkled as Grandpa's.

I take my time with dear old Dobbie. We've got lots to talk about.

After a while Dobbie shines with soft brushing and sweet talk, and I decide to see if the sale has ended.

The sky looks like a dirty chalkboard now, and I smell rain in the air.

Some folks head for their cars with stuff they've bought. There go a quilt and a lamp. Crated chickens sit in the back of a pickup. They don't look too happy about it, but then chickens never do look too happy about anything.

The tractor has a *Sold* sign on it. So do the combine and the old cream separator.

And then some stranger leads Dobbie out of the barn. Oh, no, are they going to sell him after all?

I look around at the people left in the barnyard. There's no one I know. No one to help Dobbie. Mom and Gran are inside. Dad is nowhere in sight. And Grandpa is standing way over at the edge of things, as if he doesn't belong here anymore.

"Who wants to open the bidding on this pony?" the man on the box says. "He's got a lot of good years left in him yet. Look at those strong legs and back."

Dobbie looks at me, and his big brown eyes say a lot. He doesn't want to belong to anyone else, either.

I push my way through the people. I tug at their sleeves so they'll move. Maybe it isn't polite, but this is a real emergency.

Finally I'm standing in front of the man on the box, and when I look up, he seems to nearly touch the sky.

"I'll buy Dobbie for a million billion trillion dollars!" I yell so loud that Dobbie's ears twitch.

Suddenly Grandpa is standing beside me. "Sold," he says. His face breaks into slivers of wrinkles as he smiles for the first time today. "Dobbie is sold to this young lady for a million billion trillion dollars."

A few minutes later Grandpa and I lead Dobbie back to the barn.

"Dobbie can live in our backyard," I tell Grandpa. "Because he's family and we have to stick together. But it sure was close."

"Yes, it was," Grandpa says back. "I thought I was going to lose everything."

"No way, Grandpa. Not when you've got me and Dobbie."

"I know," Grandpa says, and now he's smiling some more. "I know."

---

1. What is an auction? How does it work?

2. Has your family faced hard times?

3. How have you been able to help?

Keeping Snugly Warm

By Eileen Spinelli

It was the worst winter Niki could remember. Her father was sick in the hospital with pneumonia.

"It's no wonder!" sniffed their neighbor, Mrs. Sherman. "Your house is so cold those old lace curtains stick to the windows!"

Niki's mother had gotten a job at French's Diner, which wasn't so bad, except that the job was second shift. That meant Niki saw her mother at breakfast before she caught the school bus, but not again until almost bedtime. And she only got to visit her father on weekends.

Every evening Mrs. Sherman would bring Niki a bit of supper. Sometimes it was icky-ooky stew that had gotten cold on its way across the adjoining yards. Sometimes it was good, crunchy fried chicken. But Mrs. Sherman didn't believe in dessert, so there was never any of that.

Dessert came only when Niki's mother returned, breathless and chilly, her hair smelling faintly of smoke. She might be carrying a brown bag with two chubby donuts, a plastic container of chocolate pudding, or a quivery slice of lemon meringue pie.

Niki would have the tea water boiling, and they'd sit together on the squashed blue sofa to eat their "midnight snack," even though it was closer to nine than midnight.

Niki would tell about her day at Walden School's fourth grade. How she missed winning the spelling bee by one word. How Bobby Marino liked Marsha Wetherill. How Marsha was so stuck-up.

And Niki's mom would tell about her day. How the coffee urn bubbled over and made a mess. And how the owner's wife, Mrs. French, came in at all hours, clanking her jewelry and giving orders to all the waitresses.

And so they would grumble cozily until it really was past Niki's bedtime. Niki would finally get up and pad across the floor in her bare feet. And her mother would say for the hundredth time, "Where are your socks? Where are your slippers?"

Niki would grin and shrug her shoulders, then go upstairs and climb into bed. Her mom would make sure she was tucked in. "Are those little arms nice and warm?" she would ask, arranging the quilt around them.

"Warm as toast," Niki would say.

"Is that tummy all snugly?"

Niki would smile.

Then her mom would tweak Niki's toes. "How about those little feeties? Are they tucked in?"

Niki would giggle again at the game they had played ever since she could remember.

Next Niki's mom would read a story. And then they would say a prayer for Niki's dad. Lastly, a kiss and a hug. Niki's mom would turn off the light, and a handful of stars would nuzzle up against Niki's window, winking her slowly to sleep.

One night there was a big blizzard. Niki stood by the window, watching the snow falling dizzily down from the sky. The tea water was whistling in the kitchen. Her mother was late.

"If ever I'm late and you're scared," her mother had told her, "call Mrs. Sherman." But Niki did not want Mrs. Sherman. She wanted her mother.

The wind rattled across the yard like old bones. Niki waited. And waited.

Nine o'clock came and went.

Then 9:15 . . . 9:30 . . . 9:45 . . . 10:00 . . . 10:15.

Time piled as high as the snow outside.

At last Niki saw the red of her mother's plaid coat, blinking faintly through the swirling storm. Home! Niki threw open the door.

Her mother shook the snow from her coat. It became brilliantly red again. She draped it over the nearest chair and flopped onto the lumpy sofa, catching her breath.

"All Mrs. French's fault. Comes in last minute. 'Do this. Do that. You forgot to fill the napkin holder. Salt shaker is sticky.' I missed my bus. To top it off, the next bus got stuck in the snow."

Niki fixed the tea and set it down in front of her mother.

"Oh no!" her mother cried. "I didn't stop to get your dessert."

"That's okay, Mom," Niki said. "I'll make the dessert tonight." She scurried to the kitchen in her bare feet, but her mom was too tired to say, "Where are your socks? Where are your slippers?"

Niki made two slices of toast and spread them thick with butter. Then she sprinkled cinnamon and just a pinch of sugar on top. When Niki brought them in, her mother was almost asleep on the sofa. She reached out for a slice and took a big bite. "Mmm—delicious!"

Niki dragged the blanket from her mother's bed and tucked it around her. "Are those arms nice and warm?"

"Warm as toast," her mother said.

"Is that tummy all snugly?"

Her mom yawned and smiled.

"And how about those little feeties?"

By then her mom was too soundly asleep to feel Niki tweaking her toes. Niki didn't mind skipping her bedtime story. As she watched her mother's face relax in the cozy darkness, she said a prayer for her father by herself. Then she kissed her mother and tiptoed upstairs to her room.

Although the swirling snow hid them from view, Niki knew that a handful of stars nuzzled against her window. And against her mother's window downstairs. And against her father's window in the hospital.

And though there was no one to tuck her in this night, Niki felt snugly warm indeed.

---

1. Have you ever been worried when you're alone?

2. What have you done to stay hopeful during hard times?

3. Have you noticed that keeping positive thoughts has helped your family—and yourself?

Angelica's Own Book

By Sarah Holbrook

Angelica squirmed on the seat of the school bus. The ride back to the migrant workers' barracks seemed longer every day. At least she had her book to read.

Now that she was in third grade, Angelica could read longer books from cover to cover. But the bumpy ride made the words bounce all over the page.

Suddenly, the bus swerved. Angelica gripped the back of the seat in front of her.

"Everyone all right back there?" called the driver.

Angelica reached for her book. She gasped. "My book is gone." She fell to her knees and crawled along the grimy floor of the bus, pushing back her long, dark hair. Finally she spotted something red under a sticky lunch sack. She grabbed her book and brushed dust from the picture of the bird on the cover. Angelica pressed it against her pounding heart.

"You may keep the book for one month," her teacher had told her.

One month meant little to Angelica. She didn't measure time by clocks or calendars. She counted by crops. First there were oranges, then asparagus and strawberries, next onions, and finally cotton or tomatoes. Like migrating birds, her family moved from south to north, stopping just long enough to pick the crops.

Angelica did not want to move again. She liked her teacher. Mrs. Medina was different. She spoke Spanish. And one day, Mrs. Medina had surprised her.

"You know, Angelica, my parents were farm workers, too," Mrs. Medina had said. "We were always moving. Every summer I picked cotton in Oklahoma."

"But how did you become a teacher?" Angelica had asked.

"I made a wish," Mrs. Medina answered with a smile. "And then I worked hard to make it come true. It wasn't easy, but I never stopped thinking about it. You can make your own wish, Angelica. And then work very hard."

Angelica pictured herself holding a book and reading it to a class of children.

That night she waited for her parents to return from the fields. Exhausted, they ate their meal of tortillas and beans. Then Angelica proudly read the book to them.

"Wonderful!" exclaimed her father, giving her a hug. Angelica's mother hugged her, too, but there was a strange, sad look on her face. Why was her mother sad? Angelica thought her reading would make her mother happy.

At bedtime Angelica crawled onto her narrow cot. Her mother leaned over to kiss her and spoke softly. "Angelica, we're leaving tomorrow evening. Tell your teacher good-bye. And you must give her back the book."

The words were like cold water hitting her face. She would have to leave everything behind—the book, school, Mrs. Medina. Angelica pushed her face into her pillow and felt the sting of tears. Under her pillow she felt the precious book.

Angelica woke up before the sun rose. She saw her mother placing clothes in the box they used for a suitcase. "I want to give a present to Mrs. Medina," Angelica said.

"We don't have money for presents, Angelica. Your teacher will understand."

But Angelica kept thinking about Mrs. Medina. Suddenly she thought of the perfect gift. She would make her a book. But how? She had no paper or pencils. The only person who had paper was the crew leader. She must find him before the crew left for the fields.

Angelica ran past the concrete barracks until she came to the small frame home of Mr. Cortes, a large man who never seemed to stop yelling. She took a deep breath and knocked timidly on the door.

"What is it?" Mr. Cortes called.

Angelica considered running, but her feet felt as heavy as sacks of fruit. "I need paper, please," she said shyly. "It's important."

Mr. Cortes came to the door and stared at Angelica. "I don't have any paper," he said gruffly. Angelica did not move. "All right, here," he said, reaching behind him. "It's last month's report. That's all I have."

Angelica had almost forgotten. "And a pencil, too, please." Mr. Cortes sighed and reached for a pencil in his shirt pocket "Bring the pencil back," he said.

Angelica climbed into the back of an empty pickup truck. She worked for more than an hour, carefully printing and drawing on the back of the report. She folded the paper and tied it down the middle with a piece of twine. At last she finished, just in time to catch the bus for school.

Angelica tried all day to tell Mrs. Medina good-bye, but she couldn't do it. She read the book one last time, then left it on her desk. Under it was the book she had made and a note:

Dear Mrs. Medina, we have to leave. I hope you like the book I made. It is about a girl who grows wings and flies.

At dusk Angelica's family joined a caravan of cars and pickup trucks. As they passed the school, Angelica turned for one last look. A cloud of red dust billowed up behind the car like a thick curtain. She sighed. "I wish I had my book," she whispered.

Mother turned from the front seat and handed Angelica a small brown sack. Angelica drew in her breath. It was her book. Mrs. Medina had said, "Make a wish." Was this magic?

"But how . . . ," Angelica began.

Mother smiled. "It's a surprise. Your teacher had an older boy bring it to us. It's something she wanted you to have."

Angelica smiled. She remembered the rest of her teacher's words: "Make a wish and then work very hard." She thought about all the other books she wanted to read. For now, she would read this book again. Her very own book.

---

1. Do you have a dream for yourself?

2. What can you do to help make it come true?

3. Has an adult helped you to find your way?

Weather Report

Pointer in hand,
the weatherman stands
before the map.
"Here," he says,
tracking a thunderstorm.
"There," he says,
predicting fog.
"Forty percent,"
figuring snow squalls.
"A low, a high. . ."

But above us, the sky,
with a logic all its own
announces the sun.

Jane Yolen

Hope

Hope is something my parents hang on to:
A line between boat and dock.

For me, hope's knowing the Jell-O will jell,
believing the popcorn will pop.

My parents have hope in my medical treatments
and trust in the cure they may do.

For me, hope's a wish on a bright, falling star.
(I saw one last night. Did you?)

Marcella Fisher Anderson

Yesterday

Yesterday I knew all the answers
Or I knew my parents did.

Yesterday I had my Best Friend
And my Second Best Friend
And I knew whose Best Friend I was
And who disliked me.

Yesterday I hated asparagus and coconut and parsnips
And mustard pickles and olives
And anything I'd never tasted.

Yesterday I knew what was Right and what was Wrong
And I never had any trouble deciding which was which.
It always seemed so obvious.

But today . . . everything's changing.
I suddenly have a million unanswered questions.
Everybody I meet might become a friend.
I tried eating snails with garlic sauce—and I liked them!
And I know the delicate shadings that lie between
Good and evil—and I face their dilemma.
Life is harder now . . . and yet, easier . . .
And more and more exciting!

Jean Little

SUGGESTED READINGS • K - 6

* = PICTURE BOOK
** = MIDDLE READER

CHANGES IN THE FAMILY

*   Gauch, Patricia. *Christina Katerina and the Great Bear Train.* New York: G.P. Putnam, 1990.

** MacLachlan, Patricia. *Baby.* New York: Delacorte, 1993.

*   MacLachlan, Patricia. *What You Know First.* New York: Harper Collins, 1995.

*   McLerran, Alice. *I Want to Go Home.* New York: Tambourine, 1992.

** Spinelli, Jerry. *Maniac Magee.* Boston: Little, Brown, 1990.

LOSS IS HARD

** Day, Nancy R. *The Lion's Whiskers.* New York: Scholastic, 1995.

*   Henkes, Kevin. *Owen.* New York: Greenwillow, 1993.

*   Hughes, Shirley. *David and Dog.* New York: Prentice-Hall, 1977.

** Paterson, Katherine. *Bridge to Tarabithia.* New York: Harper & Row, 1977.

RESPECT—AND SELF-RESPECT

** Bryan, Ashley. *Turtle Knows Your Name.* New York: Atheneum, 1989.

** Henkes, Kevin. *Words of Stone.* New York: Greenwillow, 1992.

*   Hoffman, Mary. *Boundless Grace.* New York: Dial, 1995.

*   Mitchell, Rita P. *Hue Boy.* New York: Dial, 1993.

*   Velthuijs, Max. *Frog in Winter.* New York: Tambourine, 1992.

ALONE—AND SOMETIMES LONELY

*   Bang, Molly. *Goose.* New York: Scholastic, 1996.

** Byars, Betsy. *Summer of the Swans.* New York: Viking, 1970.

*   Lionni, Leo. *Alexander and the Wind-Up Mouse.* New York: Pantheon, 1969.

*   Polacco, Patricia. *I Can Hear the Sun.* New York: Philomel, 1996.

** Speare, Elizabeth. *The Witch of Blackbird Pond.* Boston: Houghton Mifflin, 1958.

ONE DAY AT A TIME

** Cheripko, Jan. *Imitate the Tiger.* Honesdale, Pennsylvania: Boyds Mills Press, 1996.

*   Karim, Roberta. *Mandy Sue Day.* New York: Clarion, 1994.

*   Lyon, George E. *Come A Tide.* New York: Orchard, 1990.

** Reiss, Johanna. *The Upstairs Room.* New York: HarperCollins, 1972.

*   Riggio, Anita. *Secret Signs—Along the Underground Railroad.* Honesdale, Pennsylvania: Boyds Mills Press, 1997.

YOU CAN DO IT

*   Polacco, Patricia. *The Bee Tree.* New York: Philomel, 1993.

** Harshman, Marc. *The Storm.* New York: Dutton, 1995.

** Paulsen, Gary. *Hatchet.* New York: Bradbury, 1987.

*   Polacco, Patricia. *Thunder Cake.* New York: Philomel, 1990.

*   Steig, William. *Brave Irene.* New York: Farrar Straus Giroux, 1986.

I DID IT

** Edmonds, Walter. *Matchlock Gun.* Mahwah, New Jersey: Troll, 1990.

*   Heide, Florence. *The Day of Ahmed's Secret.* New York: Lothrop, Lee & Shepard, 1990.

*   Kraus, Robert. *Leo the Late Bloomer.* New York: Windmill, 1971.

*   Mitchell, Rita P. *Uncle Jed's Barbershop.* New York: Simon & Schuster, 1993.

** Wallace, Rich. *Wrestling Sturbridge.* New York: Alfred A. Knopf, 1996.

THAT'S WHAT FRIENDS ARE FOR

*   Ackerman, Karen. *The Tin Heart.* New York: Atheneum, 1990.

*   Brisson, Pat. *Wanda's Roses.* Honesdale, Pennsylvania: Boyds Mills Press, 1994.

** Conrad, Pam. *Prairie Songs.* New York: Harper & Row, 1985.

** Lowry, Lois. *Number the Stars.* Boston: Houghton Mifflin, 1989.

*   Polacco, Patricia. *Chicken Sunday.* New York: Philomel, 1992.

FINDING PEACE—OR MAKING IT

*   Carson, Jo. *You Hold Me, and I'll Hold You.* New York: Orchard, 1992.

*   Hopkinson, Deborah. *Sweet Clara and the Freedom Quilt.* New York: Alfred A. Knopf, 1993.

** Hughes, Monica. *A Handful of Seeds.* New York: Orchard, 1993.

** MacLachlan, Patricia. *Skylark.* New York: HarperCollins, 1994.

*   Yolen, Jane. *Letting Swift River Go.* Boston: Little, Brown, 1992.

TOMORROW WILL BE BETTER

** Creech, Sharon. *Walk Two Moons.* New York: HarperCollins, 1994.

*   Friedrich, Elizabeth. *Leah's Pony.* Honesdale, Pennsylvania: Boyds Mills Press, 1996.

*   Grifalconi, Ann. *Darkness and the Butterfly.* Boston: Little, Brown, 1987.

** Paterson, Katherine. *Jip, His Story.* New York: Dutton, 1996.

*   Williams, Vera. *A Chair for My Mother.* New York: Greenwillow, 1982.

ACKNOWLEDGEMENTS

Every possible effort has been made to trace the ownership of each person included in *Reflections from a Mud Puddle.* If any errors or omissions have occurred, corrections will be made in subsequent printings, provided the publisher is notified of their existence.

Permission to reprint copyrighted poems is gratefully acknowledged to the following:

Lisa Bahlinger for "Moving Day." Copyright © 1998 by Lisa Bahlinger. Reprinted by permission of the author.

Curtis Brown, Ltd., for "Weather Report" by Jane Yolen. First appeared in *Weather Report.* Published by Boyds Mills Press. Copyright © 1993 by Jane Yolen; "We" by Lee Bennett Hopkins. First appeared in *Been to Yesterdays.* Published by Boyds Mills Press. Copyright © 1995 by Lee Bennett Hopkins; "Girls Can, Too!" by Lee Bennett Hopkins. First appeared in *Girls Can, Too!* Published by Franklin Watts, Inc. Copyright © 1972 by Lee Bennett Hopkins; and "Time to Play" by Nikki Grimes. First appeared in *Pass It On: African American Poetry for Children.* Published by Scholastic, Inc. Copyright © 1993 by Nikki Grimes. Reprinted by permission of Curtis Brown, Ltd.

Monica Gunning for "When Connie Died" from *Under the Breadfruit Tree.* Copyright © 1998 by Monica Gunning. Reprinted by permission of the author and Boyds Mills Press.

HarperCollins Publishers for excerpt from "Some Things Go Together" by Charlotte Zolotow. Copyright © 1969 by Charlotte Zolotow; and "Yesterday," "Alone," "Cartwheels," and "Hey World, Here I Am!" from *Hey World, Here I Am!* by Jean Little. Copyright © 1986 by Jean Little. Reprinted by permission of HarperCollins Publishers.

David Harrison for "The Test" and "I Did It!" from *Somebody Catch My Homework.* Copyright © 1993 by David Harrison; and for "First Things First" from *A Thousand Cousins.* Copyright © 1996 by David Harrison. Reprinted by permission of the author and Boyds Mills Press.

Sara Holbrook for "Here and There" from *Which Way to the Dragon?* Copyright © 1996 by Sara Holbrook; "Divided" and "Alone" from *I Never Said I Wasn't Difficult.* Copyright © 1996 by Sara Holbrook; and "Tryouts" and "Bad Joke" from *Nothing's the End of the World.* Copyright © 1995 by Sara Holbrook. Reprinted by permission of the author and Boyds Mills Press.

Marci Ridlon McGill for "The New Neighbor" and "Angry" from *Sun Through the Window*, published by Boyds Mills Press. Copyright © 1969, 1996 by Marci Ridlon McGill. Reprinted by permission of the author and Boyds Mills Press.

Jack Prelutsky for "Me I Am!" from *Me I Am!* Copyright © 1983 by Jack Prelutsky. Reprinted by permission of the author.

Marian Reiner for "The Way Things Are" from *The Way Things Are* by Myra Cohn Livingston. Copyright © 1974 by Myra Cohn Livingston. Reprinted by permission of Marian Reiner.

Simon & Schuster for "Night" from *The Collected Poems of Sara Teasdale* by Sara Teasdale. Copyright © 1930 by Sara Teasdale Filsinger. Copyright renewed © 1958 by Guaranty Trust Co. of New York. Reprinted by permission of the publisher.

Eileen Spinelli for "Moving" from *Where is the Night Train Going?* Copyright © 1996 by Eileen Spinelli. Reprinted by permission of the author and Boyds Mills Press.

University of Toronto Press for "Orders" from *Complete Poems* (2 vol.) by A. M. Klein, edited by Zailig Pollock, University of Toronto Press. Copyright © 1990 University of Toronto Press. Reprinted with permission of the publisher.

SUBJECT INDEX